SAVAGE CHASE

LION HEARTS BOOK THREE

CECILIA LANE

A SHIFTING DESTINIES NOVEL

CONTENTS

CHAPTER 1

Fuck.

The word rang through Colette Ashford's head, growing louder and louder until there was little room for any other thoughts. It drowned out the buzz of the fluorescent lights above her, the snoring of her cellmate, and most of the conversations on the other side of the thick, metal door.

Better that than picking over all the details of the night. At least the SEA agents hadn't cuffed her. The silver-plated bars were enough to keep her locked inside the holding cell. Tranquilizer guns were prob ably within reach if she decided to get rowdy.

Colette shifted on the cold bench with a grimace. No worries, there. The less movement, the better.

Fuck.

Such an expressive word. A hard, quick explosion fired off in anger. A softer whisper, followed by a harsh sigh for thinly-veiled disbelief. Said with a grimace over the buckshot still embedded under her skin.

"She took out the best of my herd! She should rot in there until they find her guilty!"

"Mr. Walsh, I'm going to need you to calm down."

"Calm down? Calm down!" Myles Walsh sputtered. "That freak has cost me thousands of dollars, and you're telling *me* to calm down?"

Colette could just about see Myles's red-faced fit. And really, she couldn't blame him. He'd ridden up to find his cattle braying in panic as a she-bear roared through them. Any rancher worth his salt would have gone on the offensive. He'd just missed some very obvious clues in the chain of events.

Hell, so had she. It wasn't until she'd arrived at the back pasture that she scented blood in the air. Nothing would have brought back the cows already dead or dying, but she'd launched herself from her saddle and let her bear take her skin in an attempt to save the rest.

She'd succeeded, but at what cost?

Colette slid her eyes closed and focused on her chant of curses, but no amount of fucks could cover the too recent and too painful memories of being yelled at, shot at, and caged in with all access for escape cut off. Somewhere in the middle of it all, they'd spotted her eyes and went for a tranquilizer gun. And poof, everything went dark until she woke in her current cell.

Her bear rolled through her with a sense of anger and frustration. She'd just been doing her job.

And trying to chase off her own personal monster.

The door leading into her wing of the Supernatural Enforcement Agency, Bozeman Branch, opened for an unexpected visitor.

Sloan Kent closed the door behind her. As an agent for the SEA, her appearance was entirely reasonable. But unless she'd been reassigned from the Bearden office, there were very few explanations why a member of her brother's clan was available for a late-night chat. None of them bode well for her plan to bury her trouble and deny its existence.

Fuck.

Colette straightened under the look of concern written on Sloan's face. "What are you doing here?" she asked anyway, hoping her brother hadn't been called. "Ethan isn't out there, is he?"

Sloan arched her brows and leaned against one of

the bars. "You want to try that one again? Maybe something along the lines of, 'Hey, Sloan, nice to see you. Thanks so much for not letting me sit in here all weekend'?"

Colette took a deep breath and pushed to her feet. She did her damnedest to keep a wince off her face and out of her step, but Sloan's eyes still dropped to her slight shuffle. "You're getting me out of here?"

"Your savior has arrived. Your brother is dealing with something calf-related tonight," Sloan said with a small shake of her head. "I talked it over with the agents here, and they've agreed to release you tonight. You're lucky they thought to give me a call. You've been ordered to appear before a judge in ten days. They're going for destruction of property, animal cruelty, endangering the lives of humans—"

"That's bullshit," Colette denied, red anger washing through her. Not the smartest choice, but her whole night had been one shitty choice after another. Pissing off the woman who, at that moment, held the key to her cage was a decision right up there with the rest of them. "If anything, he threatened me! I wasn't the one shooting wildly at anything that moved."

Sloan held up her hands and fixed her with an

impassive look. "I'm just repeating what I've been told. You will also be added to the shifter registration list and probably face some fines for working outside an enclave without proper permits."

Which would kill most chances at securing a job outside an enclave again. Colette grimaced. The one place she wanted to permanently escape had successfully tied a leash around her neck and called her to heel.

Her bear warred with her human side. Colette shoved the animal to the dark corners of her mind, but she wasn't quick enough. She was never quick enough to stop the sendings flashing through her head or the rising tide of longing that hollowed out her chest. They spoke of an impossible life that wasn't meant for her. Love and mates were lies she wanted no part of.

She blinked at the clink of metal hitting metal. Sloan swung the door of the cell open and gestured for her to exit. Colette hobbled through, doing her best to ignore the pain flashing up and down her backside.

"Tansey is collecting your things. I'd say have a little pity on the guy, but he took one look at me and asked to speak to the man in charge, so fuck him."

Colette snorted. That sounded like Myles. He

could pretend to be pleasant and all for equality, right up to the moment something went wrong. Then it was time for a big man to step in and fix things.

He wasn't the first asshole to underestimate her because of the tits on her chest, nor would he be the last. He was just the first to offer her a full-time gig after college.

She'd had dreams. Plans to build on. A life to lead. All those goals were dashed by one selfish prick who couldn't take no for an answer. But what was Myles likely to believe—the evidence of a rampaging bear right in front of his eyes or the words she spilled trying to save her ass?

Sloan walked her through the process of being released while Myles glared from the other side of the office. She signed where told, collected the few belongings she'd had on her when she went from skin to fur and back again, then stepped through the door and into the night.

She smelled him before she saw him. Colette turned her head and inhaled the piney, moonlit scent of a wolf. Her skin prickled with the push of her bear, and a growl rattled in her chest.

Headlights slashed across the parking lot, and the

dark body of the wolf disappeared around the corner of the building. Jason.

Asshole.

Tansey slid out of her truck and ran the short distance between them, wrapping her in a tight hug that had her stiffening. She pulled back, eyes scanning her frame. "Are you hurt?"

Colette put a step between them. "Nothing I can't handle," she said. Not a lie, exactly. Not the truth, either. With a wolf under Tansey's skin, Colette had to watch her words.

"Screw that," Tansey huffed. "Ethan will have my head if I bring you home harmed in any way."

"I'm fine," she insisted. She glanced over her shoulder to make sure they weren't still being watched. No eyes glowed in the darkness, but she'd rather get the hell out of there than linger.

Tansey fixed her with a no-nonsense look. "Colette…" she said with a small shake of her head. "What happened? This doesn't sound like you."

"You barely even know me," Colette snapped, then immediately turned away with a wince.

And who's fault was that? Hers.

Yet, Tansey was there when things fell apart. Sloan's connections made it possible to avoid sitting behind bars until a judge could see her. She wasn't an official member of their clan, but they still treated her like one.

Her bear stretched through her with a heavy sigh. Colette pushed back on the longing that swelled to life.

"Shit," she murmured to the ground. "I'm sorry. I'm just... exhausted. Can we head out, or is there something else needed before we go?"

"We can go," Sloan said slowly.

The two exchanged a look, which left Colette feeling on the outside.

Right where she belonged.

She could hardly remember a time when it was different. Even in school when all the other cubs had their mommies and daddies come in for career day or to share cupcakes on their birthdays, she had no one. Her mom died during a failed coup to kick the Ashfords off their own damn ranch, and her father decided life was better living drunk at all hours of the day and night. Ethan stepped up, but what did a big brother have to contribute when all the other parents talked about how awesome it was to be a police officer or firefighter or the great value of desk jobs?

She'd planned to repay him for making sure she always had food on the table or someone to help her with homework, but the last couple of years made it clear she didn't have a place on Black Claw Ranch. Mates were involved now, and cubs, too. She didn't recognize it as home anymore.

Truth be told, she didn't recognize anywhere as home. She didn't have a place to call hers or any idea where she belonged in the world. She'd tried to get her feet under her and strike out on her own, but that was an impossible dream when nowhere was safe for long.

Jason found her wherever she went.

"Will you do me a favor?" she gritted out. The words felt like driving a fork into her eye. She hated asking anyone for anything.

She was an Ashford. They got shit done on their own.

But that was another spot where she stood on the outside, now. Ethan had a mate. Hell, his entire clan had their lives sorted and buttoned up with their other halves. She was the odd one out, again.

Tansey nodded. "Of course."

The sincerity in her voice and immediate agreement made Colette feel even worse for snapping at her earlier. "Can you let me tell Ethan?"

CHAPTER 2

Dash grinned madly and paced from one side of the fighting ring to the other. He bounced his attention here, there, then rattled the flimsy chain-link that was more for show than keeping anyone in or out. He'd need more than two hands to count the times he'd seen shifters break the cage and carry their match out of the ring. Those bouts always earned the biggest cheers.

He pumped his arms into the air and worked the roar of the crowd even louder. Fucking intoxicating, that sound, but it still wasn't enough. He wanted to feel the noise skittering over his body. Loud enough, bloodthirsty enough, they'd drown out the rumblings of his inner beast.

He rolled his shoulders and punched the empty

air. He needed this. The blood, the cheers, the noise. Anything to take his mind off the last few months and dull the edge of the wanderlust gripping him and his lion.

The feeling always started in the soles of his feet. Days of discomfort worked the feeling up his legs and chest until he felt like he had ants running through his head. He'd never stayed anywhere longer than a month, tops. Not until he'd found his way to Bearden, anyway. Something—*someone*—calmed the need to move when the urge got too bad.

A rush of sendings threatened to pull Dash to his knees. He swallowed back his groan, but the mental hand he waved did little to stop the flow of too-bright images.

Colette Ashford, girl next door. Or rather, woman. Hot, sexy, mouthwatering woman. Just the thought of her was enough to set his insides on fire. She was like the damn sun, lighting up his world when she was around and plunging him back into darkness when she left.

The beast didn't leave him alone. More sendings were shoved at him. Painful, spiteful, slow-motion reels that turned his groan into a growl. Dark phone screens. Dark, cold nights. The only thing missing was a peeling of the calendar to mark the days since he'd last tasted her lips.

The message was clear. Nothing was left for him in Bearden.

Dash cracked his neck and rolled his shoulders to cut the tension welling inside him. He was stopped up. Clogged. Frustrated down to his core. He had to drain a little of the poison out before he lost control of his beast and snapped off the wrong head. A blood sacrifice was needed, and what better altar than the fighting ring?

He didn't even care who he fought. He'd scrawled his name on the board and waited to get called up. Whatever was necessary to keep from standing still, even if for just a short while. Stillness was death to his lion.

Him, too, when the door of the cage swung closed. He had to stay fast on his feet to keep upright.

Dash spun around and met his opponent head-on, ducking the blow that whistled past his ear. The man on the other end was a surprise. Welcome or not, he wasn't sure. "Aw, shit," he drawled, accent going thick with the thrill in the air, "look who's back."

Seth jabbed with his left, then his right, then his

left again, stepping forward with each punch. "You miss me?"

"Fuck no," Dash laughed. He landed a hit against Seth's side, then danced away before the other man could follow up with another blow. "Besides, don't know enough to miss."

Seth circled, predatory eyes watching for an opening to strike. "Is this where we braid each other's hair and whisper about our deepest secrets?"

"Depends. You got anything interesting to share?"

Probably not. What could be more interesting than dropping 'hey, we're products of the same scum sucking bastard, care to get a drink and talk out our shit'? He hadn't been interested in trading dream journals then, he sure as hell didn't want any brotherly bonding now.

Besides, Seth was just some guy to him. They hadn't grown up together. He hadn't known he existed until a couple months ago. The way he'd learned their old man carried on, he could fling a dart at a map and probably find another Seth within two hundred miles.

Seth lunged, sending his fist flying right for Dash's face. He jabbed forward with his own hit, landing a crack against Seth's ribs just as his head snapped back from a shot he hadn't blocked.

Dash stumbled backward, shaking his head clear. Pain throbbed along his cheek, but he grinned anyway. "Steve, wasn't it?" he taunted before diving back into the fight.

"Fucker," Seth muttered.

Dash caught him around the middle. Elbows jammed down against his shoulder to break the hold, but he gritted his teeth as he drove the man into the chain-link walls and pummeled his sides.

Fuck, yes. Unleashing on the man felt good. Right. He was made for fighting. He'd been born a tough little shit and was put to work as soon as he was big enough.

He could still remember the day his old man came to visit Mémé's and found him working over some of the other boys in their backwoods parish. Asshole hadn't put a stop to the fight in the slightest. He'd simply sat back, arms crossed, until Dash won, then rubbed his knuckles over his head.

Sometimes—before he managed to drown out his lion with booze or a brawl—he wondered what his life would have been if he'd lost that day.

Seth sent him flying backward with a hard shove. Arms windmilling, Dash laughed as he stumbled to a stop against the opposite side of the cage. "That all?"

he asked with a shrug. "Guess I know who got all the talent."

"Yeah." A cheer bathed them both as Seth threw his arms wide. "Me."

Nah. Didn't matter if he'd won or lost when he was a cub. Fate dragged them all around by the nose. Telling Waylon Asher to piss off or running far to escape his grandmother's eventual matchmaking, he'd still have found his way to Bearden.

And Colette.

Growl building inside him, he met Seth in the center of the ring. They punched wildly, blows landing as often as they caught empty air.

"Dash, Dash! He's our man! If he can't do it, no one can! Go Dash!"

He glanced up to see Hailey and Kyla standing at the top of the bleachers. Or rather, Kyla stood while Hailey balanced precariously on Trent's shoulders. Even Sage, Lindley's quiet sister, waved pom-poms with the other two wackadoos.

Last he'd heard, they were going for drinks and darts in the middle of town. He'd been disinvited when he asked if the darts had to find their way into a board, or if nailing Rhys, Lindley, or Trent in the beans counted for quadruple points. Now here they were, cheering him on.

Sappy fucks.

As much as he wanted to prove his lion wrong that he could stay in one spot, he was losing the fight. Fuck, things had been simpler before Hailey rocked up in the middle of a snowstorm. He drank and brawled and sometimes got some work done without Trent shouting out alpha orders. And yeah, the food had gotten better since Hailey claimed Trent as her own and Kyla kicked Lindley in the dick and ordered him to stop being such a mopey fuck. But he'd still had to watch them figure out their shit to keep the women crazy enough to fall for their sorry asses, all while his own mate denied his existence when she left town.

Rules, she said.

He'd gone along with that for years. She'd been in college. He hadn't wanted to mess anything up for her, make her feel like she had to choose between him and getting herself set up for life. He wasn't one of those assholes like Lindley's old pride or the fucker Trent called an uncle who needed a woman small and dependent on him for everything. He wanted a queen with fire in her belly and confidence in her every step.

But then she'd graduated and still kept him at arm's length. The woman had walls like no one else.

Thick, creeping vines wrapped around him. Dash strangled in their grasp as they blocked out the sun a little more each day. A dark voice insisted all the while that it was for the best. After all, his old man never stayed in one place. Seth couldn't be the only half-sibling out there in the world. When he already had trouble keeping still, how the fuck did he expect to treat one woman like a queen for the rest of their lives?

Except Colette was different. She was the one person who calmed his need to constantly be on the move.

Except Colette didn't want him the way he wanted her. He was fun. A distraction. Someone she could walk away from at the end of the night.

The chain-link of the cage rattled as Dash crashed against it. His lungs ached under the sudden evacuation of air. Seth landed another punch to his gut and Dash shook his head to clear the sendings and little birdies circling in a daze.

"Got yourself a nice pride there," Seth grunted after blocking a returned punch. "Been with 'em long?"

"Little insane, but they ain't so bad." He ducked under a fist coming for his face and spun around behind the man. A hard shot to the side spilled him forward, but Seth caught himself against the fencing and slammed his head back into Dash.

"Motherfucker," Dash growled, hands going to his nose. Pain lit up all his senses, but he didn't feel warmth flowing down his face. No break. Yet.

Seth whirled to meet him before he could get in another kidney shot. He threw up his hands and lashed out, but Dash was ready. He blocked and danced back, setting up for another round.

"Waylon—" Seth started.

Dash snarled. His lion roared to the front of his mind, ready to unleash claws and fangs. "Don't talk about that fucker to me."

Waylon was dead to him. Had been since the night he caught him stepping out on his mother. He didn't give a shit if that asshole still breathed or if someone had finally slit his throat. He'd never been a father. Dash couldn't even consider him a friend. Waylon was a hard, cruel, devious man only out for himself. He ruined the lives around him, drained others dry, then moved on to his next victim with glee.

Dash felt his lion's roar down to his bones. He flung himself at Seth with a savage cry of his own, frustration and stinging hurt powering his blows. A crack and a jab caught Seth square on the jaw, then his stomach. Dash didn't let up, throwing punches hard enough to force the man back.

Seth recovered a second later. Eyes flashing brightly with his inner animal, he lunged for Dash fast enough to blur. Punch, punch, jab. Balled fists slammed into flesh, the thick sounds loud even over the other man's roar.

The crowd was on their feet, their yells and screams punctuating every blow. Dash's grin slipped before widening all over again. Fucker had been playing before.

He wasn't some toy mouse to bat around the ring. He hated his legacy, but he thrived on the fights. They were in his blood.

Seth's shoulder caught his middle, and they fell to the floor together. Dash punched his head and chest and tried to slip a blow to his ribs, but they were too tangled and tight for more than a slugfest.

The world narrowed down to nothing. Sweat and blood were the only scents. Fists and pain were the only things to feel. Even the crowd faded to a dull throb of background noise while the knob on the grunts and growls of their fight twisted all the way up.

They were brutal. Feral. There wasn't anything testing or teasing in their blows now. They fought to put the other down. The win was right there, reaching for them, and whoever scrambled over the other first got to taste that tidal wave of noise swelling all around them.

Dash kicked out, but Seth was back on him in a second. Hard punches landed on his head, his ribs, made it impossible to suck down another breath before it was driven out of his lungs.

He threaded his fingers into the wire of the fence and hauled himself out from under the force working him over. Seth grabbed hold of his leg and twisted him into a submission hold, putting pressure on the break Lindley had given him a couple months ago.

Dash gritted his teeth and tried to fight through the pain that fired up and down his side. He slammed his elbow and tried to buck the man off, but Seth's grip tightened and more pressure built.

Howling, he pounded his fist into the floor of the cage.

The harsh screech of the referee called the end of the fight and Seth immediately let him loose. He bounced back to his feet and held out his hand.

Breathing hard, Dash slapped his hand into Seth's and let himself be hauled to his feet.

"Good fight," Seth said, pleased smirk hitching up his mouth.

"Fuck off," Dash answered with an equally satisfied grin. It took a hard fucker to bring him down, but he still wasn't interested in bonding with the brother he never wanted.

He raised his middle finger and limped out of the cage. He had drinks and darts and a pride of idiots waiting for him.

His lion rumbled inside him, bringing back the itch to move.

CHAPTER 3

"She emerges!" Tansey called dramatically from the kitchen.

Colette paused on the landing and considered diving back into bed, possibly forever. Maybe even a straight haul out the door, over the hills, and across the border. Running from her problems sounded much, much better than confronting them in the form of her brother's far-too-cheerful mate.

She honestly wasn't sure if the smugness in Tansey's scent was the problem. She'd finally given herself over to exhaustion in the small hours of the morning after plucking the last of the buckshot from her skin. Fitful sleep that left her feeling more gritty than rested was a strong contender for the leading cause of her desire to drive stakes through her eyeballs.

"She emerges," Colette repeated with a forced half-smile as soon as she left the final step. A prickle ran over the back of her neck and set her bear on edge.

The great room of the rechristened Ashford B&B looked the same as she remembered. Same comfy couches, maybe a few more smudges in the empty fireplace. The carved bear heads on the staircase banisters looked as ancient as ever. Pictures of the clan, the ranch and animals, beautiful skies and mountains lined the mantle or hung from the wall. She made a showing in a handful, but that number was smaller than ever.

Skies above, the place felt weirder every time she came home. At least those weekends and breaks between semesters had end dates she could eyeball and count down the days until they were over.

Now? She didn't know which way to turn.

"You hungry?" Tansey offered. "I can heat up some leftovers if you'd like."

Colette raised her hands to ward off the mothering. "I can manage to put together a sandwich. Thanks."

Which she did. And only had to open two cabinets to find the plates. Which was not frustrating in the slightest because she didn't live there anymore and had no say in where the dinnerware was housed.

Colette ducked out of the kitchen as soon as possible and retreated back to the great room. Balls. She hated the jittery restlessness that gripped her heart. Lack of sleep and feeling out of place, she told herself, denying the thinly veiled edge of excitement stemming from her inner bear. Being forced back to Bearden wasn't cause for celebration.

Her bear rolled through her with an irritated growl. Colette bit the insides of her cheeks and slammed the animal behind thick walls.

She stiffened as Ethan walked through the door.

The Ashford alpha had a commanding presence that held power over the rest of his clan, but he'd always been just a brother to her. They poked and teased each other more often than not, but the cold, blue eyes he swept over her were clear signs they were in one of the *not* stages.

Unease churned in Colette's gut as Ethan strode for Tansey and wrapped her in a tight hug from behind. The two whispered an exchange too quiet for her to hear, then her brother straightened and headed back the way he came.

"Come," he ordered as he passed, not even slowing to see if she obeyed.

Colette gritted her teeth and followed in his wake. He threw the door wide and stomped onto the porch. She shut it behind her and sank down next to him on one of the benches lining either side of the front door.

The yard was clear, though she could hear Hunter and Alex giving each other shit inside the barn. A couple horses braved the chill of late-winter snow with a chorus of distant moos from the cattle in a field out of sight. Earthy aromas and crisp air mingled together in a very specific odor that never failed to put a smile on her face and run a calming hand down her bear's back.

The scene would have been nice if not for the mountain of irritation next to her.

Colette wished he'd say something. Yell at her. Anything but sit there and stare out over the ranch. The silent treatment let her fill in the gaps, and she was in no place to treat herself kindly.

Failure. Fuck up. Criminal.

Long minutes passed before she carefully asked, "How much did Tansey tell you?"

"Not much," Ethan admitted testily. "I hope you understand the burden you put on my mate. The entire clan, actually. Tansey didn't do this on her own, Sloan wouldn't say anything, either, and Lorne was ready to fight in fur when I questioned her. You've been here roughly ten hours and you're already throwing everything into chaos."

Despite her best efforts, Colette fidgeted under his attention. She hated feeling like a disappointment even more than she hated the nervous sinking in her stomach. "I still can't believe you have a mate," she blurted.

"I didn't have much choice." He snorted, then unwound and leaned back against the house. "I either had to get over my shit, or she'd put a hole in me. The better bet was a mate match when the other option was getting my dick shot off."

Colette made a face. "Gross. I don't want to acknowledge that you have anything going on in your jeans."

"Same, sister. Same."

He'd left her behind.

It wasn't a fair thought, but it still bubbled to the surface anyway. How could it not when the evidence surrounded her? The barn had been rebuilt after a fire ravaged the previous one, and she knew he'd upgraded the space inside. The herd was bigger than ever. Trail rides and camping trips were regular offerings to the guests that booked rooms in the main house.

Ethan had done so much to bring the place back to a glory it hadn't seen since before their mother died and their father gave up on life. But *he'd* done them, not her. Not them.

They'd been aligned together and faced off against the world for as long as she could remember. It was a bittersweet sting to know she wasn't needed.

"What the hell happened, Colette?" Ethan asked. "Why did Sloan know you were in trouble, but not me?"

"I…" She trailed off, pressed her lips together, and turned her face away. She didn't want to face the disappointment written all over his features. Too bad, because it was right there in his scent and his voice. Sharp, stinging, questioning. It cut deeper than listening to Myles Walsh rage against her kind or staring down the barrel of outing herself permanently as a shifter and facing legal action.

"I fucked up," she said on a harsh breath. "There was trouble on the ranch. I tried to do the right thing, and I fucked it up and ended up in SEA custody."

"What sort of trouble?" Ethan growled low,

thickening the air around them with the force of his inner animal.

"The kind that gets you shot full of tranquilizers and charged with endangering human lives."

His growl cut off sharply. Ethan turned his head slowly to lock her in place with his stare. Deceptively calm, he asked, "Did you do it?"

"No," she answered emphatically. "Absolutely not."

"But you know who did," he said flatly. When she turned away and didn't say anything, he ground his teeth. "Colette, you have to tell someone."

"No."

"Colette—"

"No," she repeated. "Ethan, you told me my entire life to be careful about who I let see me. Our safety depended on it. That part is on me. The rest? I can't just hand someone over to the human authorities."

"This person broke the law—"

"What about our rules? Our laws?" She let off a frustrated noise. "Three strikes, right? Three strikes before the SEA interferes?"

"So this person just gets away with it?"

She shook her head. "No. No, I didn't say that. I reported him to his people. I just didn't want to get humans involved. We handle ourselves. That's what you've always said."

"That's all well and good when the party being punished isn't my sister," he growled.

"This is why I didn't want to tell you," Colette answered with a growl of her own.

That, and not wanting to feel like a burden. She'd tried to contain what she thought was a simple problem and watched it spiral out of control until it ate up her future.

Her bear paced with displeasure at the dominance rolling off her brother. Tense silence held them captive until Ethan dipped his chin once and pushed to his feet. "Okay."

Colette blinked and shook her head in disbelief. "That's it? No lecture? No demands for more information?"

"What more do you want me to say? You're grounded? I'm cutting you off?" Ethan snorted. "Those didn't work when you were still a girl. No way in hell you'll let me use them now."

"You never could ignore me for longer than a day," she chuckled. A weight lifted off her shoulders at the crack in her brother's irritation. "And I'd just sneak out anyway. The trellis under my window is surprisingly sturdy."

He nodded seriously, scent filling with amusement. "See? There's no point in trying. You're going to do what you want to do. All the rest of us can do is install climbable structures so you don't hurt yourself at the end of the night."

Colette grinned. "You did that on purpose?"

"You really weren't as slick as you thought," he deadpanned.

She scoffed and narrowed her eyes in mock anger. "I take offense to that."

"Take it up with the broken taillight of your senior year. Or the gate debacle that mixed all the calves into the herd right before they were supposed to be given their vaccines. We can't forget the greatest hits of 'the cows ate my homework' whenever you missed an assignment."

A laugh bubbled out of Colette. Skies above, it was nice to joke with him. Even her bear quieted and settled inside her. "It was real at least three times!"

Ethan turned serious again. "I think you're making a mistake, but I also know these fuckers," he gestured vaguely toward the cabins belonging to the clan, "would have been ruined if they weren't given a chance to get their shit together. There's no way I can talk you out of this?"

"No," she said with a small shake of her head.

She didn't want to push the situation, though Ethan didn't know that. She'd made sure Jason's people were informed of the years-long torment he'd put her through. They'd promised to take care of the situation. She just wanted to put it all behind her.

"Stubborn bear," he griped. "It's good to have you home."

"I learned it from you," she taunted, her smile not as broad as before. Home. That one word made her feel like she stood on the outside all over again. Colette rolled her shoulders and shoved her bear down deep before disappointment soured her scent.

Ethan rolled his eyes and stomped down the front steps. "Get a job," he called over his shoulder. "I don't want you bumming around my ranch longer than necessary."

"Does meeting up with Tawny count?"

Ethan stopped. Hands on his hips, he peered up at the sky, then slowly shook his head. "All the gods in the sky won't save us now," he muttered.

CHAPTER 4

D ash couldn't breathe.

Well, that was a damn lie. His lungs worked just fine. In, out, inhale, exhale. Air moved in, worked magic disguised as science on his blood, and zipped through his limbs. The physical part wasn't the problem.

"Hurry up, Dash!" Kyla called over her shoulder. "Last one has to buy the first round!"

Shit. He glanced across the parking lot and past the packed barbecue joint on the other side of the road. The darkness called to him and his inner lion. Mysteries resided in the shadows and inky blackness. And wouldn't it be better to cut ties with everything now, before he fucked it all up?

Move, his body and his beast urged.

He'd stayed in one place for too long. Even the air weighed on him. And all for what? Nothing was going to change. He'd fuck up his spot in the pride before long. She wasn't coming back.

Dash growled and jogged after the group. He punched Rhys in the side, then elbowed ahead of Lindley. His hand latched around the door handle a fraction of a second before Trent's.

"I'm not buying you fucks anything," he drawled, throwing a grin over his shoulder as he stepped inside The Roost.

Noise rolled over him. Glasses clinked, cue balls thunked against others on the pool tables, patrons gasped and groaned as the storytellers in their groups worked out the kinks of their weeks. The scents of booze and bar food should have soothed his cranky animal, but the urge to leave it all behind had his heart in a fist.

Fucking Seth. Fucking Waylon. Like he needed to hear the name after leaving that miserable old fuck behind years ago. He especially didn't want to hear it from the asshole who showed up and rocked the boat, then pulled a disappearing act just like their old man.

Dash pulled to a sudden stop, the highlight reel of complaints going static in his brain. His lion sat up with renewed interest that had nothing to do with blood and brawls.

He inhaled deeply, then grinned. Aw, yeah. The night had taken a turn for the better.

Fresh forest scents mingled with unique spices he could only compare to cinnamon and spirits. Tangy, with the right amount of burn to keep him coming back for more. He parted his lips to draw more of the delicious scent into his lungs and exhaled a pleased growl.

Dash swept his gaze over the bar and settled on a dark corner in the back. There she was. Colette Ashford, girl next door. Only, Colette was no girl. She was grade-A, dick-hardening, gorgeous woman.

She even had one of those pretty names that hid a spine of steel and take-no-shit attitude just like all the girls his grandmother used to run wild with in her younger days. Elodie. Genevieve. Madalina. The way he craved Colette, he could almost believe she'd worked some of that old swamp magic on him.

He consumed her slowly, taking in the cowboy boots on her crossed ankles and the inches of smooth skin he wanted to lick and nibble until he reached the hem of her cutoff shorts. Her top wasn't anything special—plain black that caressed her curves without hugging tightly and offered a modest peek of cleavage instead of baring all to the world. Light blonde hair hung past her shoulders, the ends twisting with the tiniest hint of curl that he always wanted to wrap around his fingers.

She was here. She was back home.

She wasn't alone.

His lion roared through his head. Sendings flashed. Hot blood on his tongue, red spilled on the floor. The beast under his skin slashed and shoved at him, aching to tear apart the male handing a fresh drink to his mate.

A hand shoved hard at him from behind, breaking his gaze. "Keep moving, asshole," Lindley grumbled.

Dash growled over his shoulder and shuffled aside. "Step on through, your holy knob goblin," he snarked.

When he glanced back to the corner, Colette had hopped off her barstool. Tawny, her friend and fellow troublemaker, leaned a little too heavily against the wall at her back. No matter, because another man stood near, his fingers running up and down her arm as she smiled slowly up at him.

Fuck. *Fuck.* Dash rubbed the heel of his hand over his heart. The itch in his feet flamed up his legs, his spine, and into his brain. He didn't want to watch Colette on a date.

But when he turned to get the hell out, he nearly ran into Rhys coming through the door. And then Hailey quirked an eyebrow at him and Kyla giggled at whatever he'd called Lindley. Even Sage had a small smile, and hell if he'd be the one to take that from her or put up with Rhys acting pissy for the next ten and a half years for upsetting her.

Fucking trapped when all he wanted to do was bail out of Bearden and find some new hellhole to terrorize until his feet started to itch again.

Dash grimaced as the pride made their way to the bar for the first round of drinks. Leah, one of the main bartenders, took a single look at them, then down the bar to her dragon boss, Gideon.

"No fighting!" they shouted in unison.

Drink in hand, Dash cursed all the gods in the sky when the only open pool table happened to be right next to Colette and her group.

"Registration isn't so bad," he heard Tawny say in an overly reassuring tone. She accompanied the words with a hand slapped onto Colette's thigh. "You can get declined, sure, but I wouldn't want to work somewhere I can't be myself. Really weeds the assholes out just as much as the supes."

"Ladies," he greeted, drinking in Colette all over again.

Her face lit up as soon as her eyes landed on him. Fucking hell, they were his favorite color. Bright, clear blue like some fantasy beach location. That look stroked a soothing hand over his jealous beast's back and calmed the possessive urges to rip those other males to shreds.

"Dash!" she exclaimed, too loud even for the bar. She scrambled off her seat and threw herself against him for a staggering hug that was over too soon. "What are you doing here?"

"I could ask you the same thing. I thought you had some fancy job down south." He flicked a glance at the men and inhaled sharply. One was human, the other something small that made his lion eager to give chase. Either way, the beast wanted to snarl and warn both away from his mate. He settled for the glares thrown in his direction.

"You better," Tawny hiccupped, "you better watch out. Colette is a hardened criminal now."

"Shhh," Colette giggled. She tried to cover Tawny's mouth and hit her nose instead, pulling a matching giggle from her friend.

"Oh yeah? Spend some time behind bars?" Dash smirked. Damn. She usually kept her shit together better than this. Watching Colette dead-ass drunk was the highlight of his day. "What did you do, rob a Girl Scout stand?"

"No!" Tawny leaned in conspiratorially. "She likes her cows *raw.*"

"Rude! Tawny, rude!" Colette scolded. She lunged to cover her friend's mouth again, then tumbled against her side that took them both down in another peal of laughter.

The two vultures threw him another glare. The chew toy shifter swooped in and pulled Tawny off the stool and back into the game, playfully helping her line up her shot while laying his claim with a generous amount of touching. The other half of the duo took Tawny's spot and distracted Colette into conversation. Asshole even threw a smug smile over her shoulder.

Dash gave a small shake of his head and resisted the urge to bare his teeth. He shoved his lion behind bars as thick as his wrist to keep the creature's possessive desires contained.

She wasn't his mate. Not in the proper sense of the word. He hadn't put his mark on her skin. She could go out with any damn person on the planet.

Trent stepped into his line of sight. Hard eyes bored into his. "This is supposed to be a nice night."

"Then we should have left the kids at home," Hailey teased as she passed, grabbing the shortest stick from the brackets mounted on the wall.

Dash grunted. He didn't need alpha power to tell him to back down and not make a scene. He leaned against the wall and took a swig from his beer bottle, eyes never leaving Colette.

The human brushed his fingers over her cheek and tucked her hair behind her ear. "You want to get out of here?"

Colette shrugged out from under his arm. "I want to take my turn."

He followed after her as she stalked around the pool table, standing too close for Dash's tastes. Colette's, too, if her frown was to be believed.

Colette leaned over and lined up her shot. She drew back, flicking a look over the far edge of the table that grabbed him by the balls, then sent the cue ball flying with a sharp jab.

The human stepped up behind her. Startled, Colette jerked upright. His hand went around her waist to drag her closer.

Anger flashed through her eyes. That was all Dash needed. He threw his pool cue to the table, spinning balls out of their spots and rattling complaints out of his pride. He didn't hear a damn thing but the blood pounding in his ears as he closed the distance to Colette.

He snapped a hand around the dickhole's arm and wrenched him around. His lion slashed and paced through his head, firing off vicious sendings of blood and death. His gums ached with the press of fangs and his fingernails darkened.

"Dash," Colette hissed, trying to pry him away from the human. "What are you doing?"

Silence rippled through the bar. Eyes turned their way, mouths zipped closed. Silence rippled through the bar, then everyone exploded into action.

Trent, Lindley, and Rhys were suddenly at his side. Tawny stumbled to Colette. The human's friend wedged his way into the mix and everyone had something to fucking say.

"Dash."

"Stop this."

"What's going on?"

"Leave," Dash ordered. He kept his snarl locked on the human and pulled on his inner animal enough to flash his eyes gold.

"But—" the human started. His cheeks paled under the sheer weight of dominant energy spiraling through the bar.

"Leave," he gritted out, "before everyone here knows you can't keep your hands to yourself."

The shifter tugged on his friend's. The sour scent of fear burst into his scent. "Let's go," he said. "They're not worth the fight."

Colette narrowed her eyes. "Excuse me?"

He scoffed. "Like you were going to suck his dick the way you've been eye fucking this one since he walked through the door."

A low growl rattled in her throat. Eyes blazing bright silver, she threw all her weight into a punch that snapped the shifter's head back.

Dash grinned madly as all hell broke loose. Hands grabbed him, Colette, the rest of the pride. The shifter and human duo were caught up in the mix, too, but unfortunately kept too far for any direct hits. That didn't stop him from trying to claw his way toward the fuckers who dared mistreat his mate.

Or from her trying to yank free and go after the bastard with blood running down his face.

Words, actions, he didn't know which he hated more. One thing for certain, seeing her throw a punch and start a brawl to defend herself was damn sexy.

"Hey!" Leah shouted over the fray. "Cut the shit!"

"Now!" a deeper voice commanded in a tone loud enough to rattle the windows and shake the bottles and glasses on the table.

Everyone stilled.

Smoke trailed from Gideon's nostrils as he stepped up next to his bartender. The dragon swept a furious look over the crowd before zeroing in on Dash and the rest of his pride.

Jerking his thumb toward the door, he snarled one word. "Out."

CHAPTER 5

Dash loaded himself behind the wheel of his truck and cocked an eyebrow at his remaining passenger. He'd made sure those asshole males from the bar skedaddled back to whatever mud puddle they'd squirmed out of, then chaperoned Tawny into her brother's care.

Just him and Colette, now. Quiet anticipation hummed along his skin.

She was home. Right there, a foot from him at the most.

His lion rolled to his back, paws flung in the air. Damn beast acted like he'd spent the afternoon face planted in the good catnip.

Not that he was much better. Each breath dragged more of her scent deep into his lungs. His heart kicked to life and his fingers twitched to reach across the truck and touch her silky skin. Fuck, he'd missed her. Her biting words and laugh hidden underneath. Hell, that attitude that didn't take shit even from strangers. She made the rest of the world bearable.

He fired up his engine and pulled back onto the main road. Silence wrapped around them both as the lights of Bearden's main drag disappeared into the darkness.

Dash stole another look at Colette. "Where to, miss?"

Home. Definitely home. As much as he wanted that to be his den, she was in no state for all the dirty things he wanted to do to her. He had to content himself with her scent and physical presence in the seat next to him.

Colette started. She blinked bleary eyes as a wan smile washed over her face. "Oh, I don't know. Anywhere but here."

The words were said with a twinge of sadness he didn't expect from her. Dash furrowed his brows, trying to watch her and the road at the same time. "Does that have something to do with what Tawny was talking about? You being a hardened criminal?"

She settled her cheek on her fist and eyed him for

a long moment. For a second, he thought she might answer. Might let him in.

Then her scent shifted. The light, tangy spices turned sour. Her bright blue eyes shuttered. He could just about feel individual bricks being slammed down as a wall grew up between them.

His lion rumbled with displeasure. Claws bit into him, slashing at his middle and sinking straight into his brain.

She shook her head and quietly asked, "What are you doing?"

"I'm trying to talk. Catch up. You know, what people do when they unexpectedly meet in a bar after months of silence." He tacked on a joke to soften the words. "You owe it to me. I'm missing pool and dart night. I was promised at least three stabbings before you got us kicked out."

"Me?" she rolled her head against the seat and fixed him with an unsteady glare. "You started everything."

"I don't recall throwing the first punch. That was all you, ma'am." And still sexy as hell. "What were you even doing with those clowns?"

"We have rules, Dash," she sighed. "Tawny's idea, anyway. I would have been happy without the extra company."

"*You* have rules," he corrected lightly. His lion relaxed a fraction. At least the fuckers weren't competition he'd have to bury a few hundred miles away. "I have principles. And I won't let some dick wart get handsy with anyone unwilling."

"Dick wart," she huffed a laugh, then descended back into silence.

She stared out the window for another long moment, scent swirling with a dull mix of emotion he didn't even want to guess at and all the drinks burning through her system.

A smile twitched the corner of her lips and slowly widened until mischief sparkled in her eyes. Colette unclicked her seatbelt and leaned closer to rub her cheek against his shoulder.

His lion rumbled in his head, loving the female marking him as hers. Sendings flooded his mind, but Dash shoved them all away. He didn't need his inner animal when his own imagination stitched together memories of Colette, naked and stretched out under him, cheeks flushed, his name on her lips.

She pressed her hand to his stomach. His cock punched hard against his jeans the moment she let off a soft growl and nipped his neck. Heat blazed under his skin as she dragged her hand lower and lower until she reached his bulge.

"Fuuuuck," he hissed, eyes rolling to the back of his head. Dash bit his lip and squeezed his hands around the steering wheel to keep from reaching for her. "You need to stop doing that, baby."

"Why?" she purred. "This is what we do."

And she was right. Two and a half years, maybe a little more, they'd done this dance. Nothing serious, rarely anything overnight. She lived her life, he lived his, and they sometimes crossed paths when she came home from college. She kept her walls up and him locked on the outside even when they were completely bare otherwise.

Rules.

Well, rules were made to be broken. He knew who he wanted, who his lion hunted. He was a bad match for her—for anybody—but he didn't give a shit. He wanted more than single nights with her.

"Colette, darlin', if you'd had maybe five gallons less and not gotten into a bar fight." She squeezed his dick and he let off a helpless groan.

Sweet skies above. His gums ached with the press of fangs and all he could think about was pulling over, ripping those shorts down her legs, and sliding into her slick heat. Her scent was thick enough, hot enough, that he knew what she wanted. No, *needed.*

With a growl, he grabbed her wrists between his

and maneuvered her back into her seat. "Okay," he said in a choked voice. "Safety first. Seatbelt on at all times."

She stuck out her lower lip in a coy little pout, but complied.

The rest of the drive was an agonizing study in patience and virtue. His lion wanted her. He wanted her. And her delicious, addicting scent lured him in with every breath he took. It was almost a blessing when he killed the engine in front of the Ashford house and stepped back into the chilly night to help Colette wobble to the door.

He watched her stab wildly at the lock with her keys before shaking his head. "How much did you have to drink?"

She shrugged. "I wasn't counting."

"I'm sure that fuckface was happy with that," he grumbled. Gently, he pulled her keys from her hand and slid the key into the lock.

The door swung open on an empty great room. The lamp nearest to the door had been left on, along with the flowery piece dangling over the sink. Even so, the place felt homey and lived in. He could almost feel ghosts passing through him as they carried on in their cheerful memories.

He hadn't felt that since leaving Mémé's and

joining his old man on the road. Motels—when they could afford them—were temporary stopovers. They didn't feel like a home.

Colette stumbled taking the first step and caught herself against the handrail. Dash sprang to her side, warmth flaring under his palms the moment he wrapped his hands around her arms. Lion purring at the touch, he murmured quietly, "Let me help you upstairs."

"I can do it."

"Breaking your neck out of sheer stubbornness. Is there a more Colette thing to do?"

She snorted and shoved her shoulder against him. He bent at the exact moment, letting her tumble right into his scooped arms.

Dash grinned down at her. "Well, ain't this just perfect?"

Colette shook her head with a silent laugh, then pointed up the stairs. "Onward, valiant steed."

"Holy hell. You are going to hurt in the morning." Shifter metabolism worked great to burn off alcohol, but still overloaded if fed a continuous stream of booze. He should know. He'd had plenty of experience waking up to death o'clock.

Dash followed the thin, alluring trail of Colette's scent up the stairs, down the hall, and to a door at the far end. He nudged it open with Colette still snuggled against his chest.

She squinted up at him with a warm smile that made his heart thump. "You shouldn't be here," she teased.

Damn right. Rules. This was her space and strictly off-limits. Was it any wonder why? The private, guarded Colette couldn't hide in her own room.

Pictures edged her mirror, most looking like they'd been placed there before she went away for college. He recognized some of the faces of Bearden residents, like Tawny and the Old Maids. Two frames sat on either side of her dresser. One showed her and her brother, Ethan, grinning from horse-back. The other was a family portrait with an older man resting his hand on a young boy's shoulder and a woman cradling a tiny baby in her arms.

He cleared his throat and tore his eyes away as his lion stretched uncomfortably under his skin.

Boxes sat in a lopsided stack in one corner. The top was thrown off and the clothes inside looked as picked through as the poorly hung mess inside the half-opened closet.

Dash glanced back to the woman in his arms. Maybe she'd had an off night. Or maybe those boxes had been pulled from storage and she hadn't had time to go through them. But combined with her sad words and wild side, the mess scratched at him that something was wrong.

He flipped the moss green blankets over to the side as much as possible with his hands full of unsteady woman. "Down you go," he warned, settling her against the pillow. He sank down at the end of the bed and drew her legs over his lap. He tugged at the heel of one shoe. "You shouldn't be in town."

"Not my choice," she declared with a finger waved through the air like a sword.

Her first boot dropped to the floor. "And you just rolled over and came back?" Dash clicked his tongue. "That doesn't sound like you, baby."

She rolled her eyes hard enough to loll her head to the side. "I'm not a baby."

He tugged off her second boot. "No? How about Medusabeast? Horseface? Or are you looking for a hardcore, biker name like Bonesaw or Blade? Maneater might be better. I've seen you work those fists."

Colette's smile widened as he yammered on. "He shouldn't have questioned my worth."

"You're priceless," Dash said quietly. Whatever

had brought her home, whatever bothered her to sadness, he wanted to fix.

She rolled to her side and tucked her fist under her chin. Her eyes drooped closed. "Thank you for getting me home."

It took everything in him not to reach for her. He wanted to feel the heat spark under his palms when he ran his hands down her side and dragged her closer to him. His mouth watered for the taste of her, already anticipating the explosion on his tongue.

Bite. Mark.

Mate.

Dash swallowed his groan as he shoved back on his lion's urges. He teetered on the edge of something, swaying from the whiplash of the night. He'd been prepared to flick the Crowley pride one last middle-fingered salute before kicking the dust of Bearden off his boots.

Now? Now, he had another chance to keep his lion steady. Another shot to make Colette his.

Never in his life had he so badly wanted to not fuck up.

Dash leaned down. Fuck, she smelled so good. He dragged his nose up the column of her neck. His lion shoved at him for *more.* A taste. *More.* A claiming.

He pressed his lips to the soft spot under her ear and yanked back on his inner beast when she let off a tiny whimper. Tempting to crawl into bed next to her, but he'd stayed gentlemanly while she grabbed his dick. Best not ruin his streak so soon.

"Dream well," he told her, then straightened.

Fuck, he'd need an ice bath when he got home.

CHAPTER 6

D eath would have been a mercy.

Colette pulled her pillow over her face to drown out the clinking of cutlery on plates from the kitchen below. She never hated her superior hearing more than when a sudden peal of laughter launched an attack on her senses.

She blindly threw her hand out for her phone and came up empty despite multiple pats in the general vicinity. Frown pulling at the corners of her mouth, Colette yanked the pillow off her face and sat up.

Bad move. The room rocked and spun. A violent shudder ran down her spine as her head revolted against the sudden lurching.

Balls. She hadn't been so hung over in, well, ever.

She threw a look around her room. Her boots were neatly arranged against the wall by the door. Her keys sprawled in a twisted pile that matched her insides and served as a reminder of needing a ride into town for an early morning drive of shame to pick up her truck.

Holy crap. She'd punched a guy.

That didn't need to make its way back to Ethan.

Colette let her head droop with a sigh, then startled straight as her pocket buzzed. So her escort home hadn't gone diving into her pockets. That was very... respectful of him.

She swiped away the notifications of a weather update—one last snow for the season was likely—and emails that were destined for the junk folder. That left a voicemail from the lawyer she'd called on Sloan's recommendation and promptly ignored while she was meeting Tawny for dinner before their night of drinking, and a text from Dash.

Let me know you're alive.

Alive? Only by the technicality of still breathing.

A wave of guilt twisted with the sour feeling in her stomach at the unanswered messages above his last.

You missed the Old Maids beating someone with their purses today.

Anyone home?

You left without a proper goodbye, baby.

Her bear shot off with a grumpy growl. The beast hated seeing those messages, but Colette had resisted responding. What good would it have done with the miles and miles between them? She didn't want to lead him on when the only thing she could offer was some harmless fun while she was in town.

Sendings flashed through her head, rocking back and forth as dramatically as her reality. Dash took front and center, eyes as bright as ever with plans sure to piss someone off. Warmth spread through her middle as he yanked his shirt over his head. Her bear shoved at her hard enough to make her gums ache in desperation to mark the man as her own.

Colette growled and kicked her bear to the back of her head. Nope. Nuh-uh. Not happening.

A whole lot of crazy had been thrown her way over the last two years. She didn't know how many times she'd moved and tried to hide herself while she finished up school. She thought she'd been safe when she took the job on a human ranch, but she should have known better.

She needed to get her feet back under her and she couldn't do that if she let her bear run wild with impossible daydreams.

A mate? A mate was trouble she couldn't afford.

But holy hell, did Dash make resisting a hard thing to do. One dirty smirk was all it took to make her melt in the palm of his hand, and Dash very rarely left it at just hands.

Colette quickly typed out an answer. *I'm alive. Thanks for the ride home.*

That was safe enough.

Colette connected her phone to the charger, then pushed herself out of bed and into her morning routine. Just because she'd swallowed down her weight in alcohol and felt like the rough side of a sheet of sandpaper didn't mean she should stay in bed all day.

By the time she made it downstairs, only two couples remained at the table. Tansey sat across Ethan's lap and shared pieces of bacon with him while they both made gooey eyes at the other family.

Joss and Hunter took turns trying to ply their small cub, Jackson, with bits of scrambled eggs. The boy screeched and slammed his hand into the spooned offering, then gurgled and tried to pick up the pieces that landed on his highchair tray.

Colette's stomach turned against her. She spun around and slipped out the door, unsure if the happy couples or the hangover made her want to puke.

Probably the happy couples.

Colette sank down on a bench and stretched out her legs. The chill of the morning felt good against her skin and the crisp air cleared her nose. She suddenly felt silly and useless for forcing herself out of bed so early when she didn't have a job to get to. Her biggest item for the day was returning the lawyer's phone call and she couldn't do that for a handful of hours. There wasn't really a whole lot of relaxing to be done while a sword dangled over her.

Balls.

She cocked her head at a distant rumble, then perked up when she heard the familiar clank of tires bouncing over the cattle grate at the end of the ranch road. Soon, a mud-splattered truck roared into the yard and slammed to a stop.

Colette wiped the smile off her face as Dash dropped to the ground. "What are you doing here?" she asked.

He threw her a wink, then leaned back into his truck. He reemerged with two big travel mugs in his hands. "I brought coffee. Figured you might need a little pick-me-up after last night."

"You didn't need to do that," she protested.

Her bear hummed in pleasure as long strides carried him closer. Colette didn't have the strength to push back against the beast, especially when he brought her the very thing she needed to feel somewhat alive.

He was tall, with grey eyes that nailed her in place. He'd shaved lines into the already short trim on the sides of his head, but left the top longer and perfectly mussed. His voice sent shivers down her spine. Rich and deep, with an accent that thickened when he got excited. Hearing him whisper dirty, sexy things in her ear was a sure way to push her over the edge.

His light, long-sleeved shirt clung to him like a second skin. He'd left the top buttons popped open. Only thing sexier, in her opinion, would have been if he'd rolled up his sleeves and let those forearms out into the world.

His jeans hung low and offered the slimmest peek of skin on his hips. Hips she knew were defined with tight lines of muscle that made just about everyone go a little stupid. Those weren't the only ones, either. She'd spent time licking the indentations between his abs, his arms bulged with strength, and she could bounce a quarter off his exquisitely defined backside. The man was one scrumptious, carefree package.

"Shit, I got them mixed up." Dash made a face at

the mugs in his hand, one eye closed as he lifted and lowered them in consideration. He took a quick swig of one, then passed it to her with a sour look. "That's yours."

Colette tipped the drink in a silent toast, then carefully sipped the contents. Her eyes widened, and she sputtered, "Is this coffee or pure alcohol?"

"Aw yeah," he grinned, accent thickening slightly. "Should have warned you. Hair of the dog that bit ya will help clear that head of yours."

Dash took a seat next to her and pulled a flask from his hip. Popping the top of his coffee, he added a good measure of amber liquid, then slipped the flask back into place. "So," he started casually, "how did your night go?"

Colette covered her face with her hand. "I don't want to talk about it."

Embarrassment oozed out of her. She'd punched a guy. In the middle of a bar. All because he dared to get mouthy with her.

Temper, temper. Last time she'd lashed out led to getting her ass handed to her by a rifle full of buckshot and a dart packed with drugs.

Her inner bear let off a low growl. She definitely didn't want to talk about being fired and winding up as roomies with her big brother and his stupidly happy clan.

"Talking ain't your style."

Dash spoke to the air, but darted a quick glance in her direction. His lips twitched with another grin. His scent—baked earth, fresh soap, and spices that made her bear lick her lips—filled with mischief that dared her to play.

"No, but apparently making an ass of myself is, so…" Colette shrugged and took another swig of her doctored coffee. Warmth spread through her, burning away the worst of her raggedness.

Maybe there was something to the hair of the dog theory. It'd always sounded like a load of junk to her, but the aching in her joints and throbbing in her head faded away like tight muscles going up against a hot bath. Even her bear settled inside her head.

"Are you kidding? You were great! Trent's probably going to hang a plaque in your honor." A corner of his mouth hitched up in a lopsided smile. "For once, we weren't the only ones kicked out of the bar!"

"Not the claim to fame I wanted," she said dryly.

"Own it. Nothing better than a woman who stands up for herself." His eyes sank down her frame before slowly roving back to her face. "You going to be around for a while?"

Colette ran her thumb up and down the side of her mug and pressed her lips into a thin line. "Seems that way."

"Good." Dash bounded to his feet and backed against the railing directly across from her. Dark grey eyes stroked down her frame as he took a drink from his mug. "So you'll have time to grab dinner with me."

Colette let off a startled laugh. "That sounds like a date."

Which was strictly off-limits. No dates. No formal titles. She had to protect herself from temptation. Love, mates, poison.

But… he was a sight for sore eyes. Dash was rough, rugged, and always had a smile and a scheme to make the day fun. She doubted he had a serious bone in his body, which was exactly what she wanted when she was in Bearden.

"Maybe it is, maybe it isn't." He shrugged. "I already had to beat two guys off to keep you to myself."

"Do you do that often? Beat guys off?" She coolly took a sip of her drink, eyeing him over the rim.

Dash barked a laugh. "Fuck that, baby. You know how I swing."

Oh, did she ever. Red flushed her cheeks while fire licked through her veins.

The front door creaked open and out stomped her brother, cutting off whatever clever retort that had been burned right out of her head.

"I thought I heard someone drive up," Ethan said. He turned a hard frown on Dash. "Lion."

"Bear," Dash greeted with a toothy grin.

"Does your alpha know you're here?"

Dash scoffed. "I don't need his blessing to be here."

"No," Ethan growled. "You need mine."

Colette rolled her eyes and pushed to her feet. "Put your dicks away," she told them with a shake of her head. "It's too early for a pissing contest."

"Okay, okay, I'm gone." Dash raised his hands in surrender, backing away from Ethan. As soon as he reached his truck, he pointed to her. "So how about that date, maneater?"

Colette laughed as Ethan's scowl deepened. Dash couldn't be serious. A date? A real date?

"Not a chance," she shot back.

She expected something back from him. A joke, a

wink, anything but the crestfallen look that flashed over his expression.

Or the sudden ache in her heart and roar of her bear.

Silent, he loaded himself behind the wheel and roared out of the yard.

Colette cocked her head and watched his truck disappear.

What in the damn hell? He knew the rules. *She* knew the rules! Nothing had changed, despite her bear slashing at her insides.

Ethan raised an eyebrow at her. "All good?"

"Yeah," Colette said. She glanced down and, shit. She still had Dash's mug in her hand.

Her bear perked up at the excuse to see the man again.

The confusing man.

CHAPTER 7

N*o.*
No.

Well, technically, 'not a chance'. Which was as good as a 'no' because she'd laughed while she said it like she didn't think he was serious.

He was deadly serious.

No.

Not even an excuse like washing her hair or being similarly busy with whatever women got up to with their nighttime routines. Nothing about already having plans and needing a rain check. Just a handful of letters set together and punched right through his heart.

No.

Fuck. Dash's phone buzzed with a text. Feeling

hopeful, he yanked it out of his pocket, then growled when he saw the contact name.

Fuck, *no,* he did not want to deal with brother shit.

With a growl, he dropped out of his truck. Lindley and Rhys had already gathered and started the day's work. Which, naturally, included standing around and gossiping like they were auditioning to be part of the crew of nosy old boars that terrorized the town.

"Where the hell have you been?" Lindley snapped. "You should have been here a half-hour ago."

"Oh, because thirty minutes is going to kill the day's schedule. Trent's not even here yet." The rumble of a truck reached his ears as Trent drove slowly down the ranch road. Dash smirked at Lindley, flicked him off, and strode for the barn doors.

His lion paced through him, tail lashing from side to side. He hoped the others would stir the pot. A brawl or three sounded just right when his chest ached from the sudden evacuation of all his organs.

No, her voice rang through his head.

His feet itched with the urge to keep walking on and on and on until he couldn't see a sign for

Bearden anywhere. Not a tourist pamphlet. Not a whisper of the place. Just... leave.

Maybe he'd work the circuit. He could fight his way across the country, doling out and taking beatings until his head and heart were numb. The smaller the venues, the better. He wanted broken down, filthy joints to suit his dark mood.

The others followed him inside. Dash wanted to bite them.

Horses tossed their heads in their stalls as he stalked past. Good beasts, solid beasts, they were accustomed to shifters moving from one form to another. Even so, the agitation rolling off him made them spin and whicker nervously in their stalls.

Trent grabbed the halter of his big, black beast of a stallion. Ozzy, he called the thing. Hellbeast would have been more appropriate. The Crowley alpha ran a calming hand down the horse's neck and pulled his arm out of the way right before he had a chunk taken out of him.

"Dash," Trent began, irritation lacing his voice, "care to tell me why fence posts and wire were leaning against the tack room door this morning?"

"Couldn't say," Dash answered with a shrug. "Maybe ask one of the others who tried to put that shit work on me last minute yesterday."

Rhys scowled in his direction. "You broke it, you fix it."

"You were there, too. You all were." He tightened his fists and rolled his head on his shoulders. The buzz in the air pulled at his inner beast. "Or did you suddenly forget we all got out of here quick?"

"Enough," Trent growled. He passed a hand down his face. "Lin, get started checking the troughs. Rhys and Dash, saddle up. I want to know what other repairs we need before the herd gets turned out for spring grazing. I'll throw out the bales for the day and make the patch in the fence before the bears chew my ass out."

"Too late for that, I think," Lindley said with a shiteating grin. "Mind telling the class where you were this morning, Dominic?"

He growled and shoved a finger toward the pride's second. "Don't call me that."

"Dominic and Colette, sitting in a tree, K-I-S-S-I-N-G—"

Trent pinched the bridge of his nose between his fingers and scowled. "Dammit, Dash. You're not supposed to go near her. I won't have our business with the bears soured when you get tired and move on to someone new."

"Yeah, but when has he ever listened?" Rhys asked with a smirk.

Dash snarled. Bored? Of Colette? She was only the most interesting woman he'd ever come across. She made him work for every laugh and sigh and flush.

And she didn't want him.

Hurt sliced through him as sharply as the claws of his inner beast. "Yeah, well, don't worry your pretty little head about that. She's not interested."

Leave. He needed to leave. His mate didn't want him. His pride were a bunch of assholes who didn't know when to leave well enough alone. Why the fuck did he even want to stay?

His lion stretched through him. His bones ached; his muscles tightened. Even the air pressing against his skin felt like agony as he teetered on the edge of a swift change. His beast wanted out.

Heavy silence from the pride was the only answer for a long second before Rhys muttered, "Shit."

Yeah. Shit. Add a fuck and a damn to the mix, too. He hated the eyes focused on him. All the stupid pity made him want to claw them up. His insides bubbled and boiled like a witch's cauldron, but the only thing brewing was a load of dark, stinging anger that needed somewhere to go.

"Yeah," he said lightly. He flicked a glance at Rhys. Easy pickings. "Now I can join the ranks of the truly sad and unhinged. You think Sage will bat those pretty eyes at me, too?"

Rhys's eyes flashed bright silver with his inner lion. His lips peeled back in a snarl as he lunged for him.

Fuck, yes. Finally.

He needed to push it all out of his system. Needed the breath of calm he felt after wringing himself of his fury.

No.

Dash danced backward, mouth spreading into a grin. "Bring it, peckerhead."

Fists flew into his ribs, his stomach. He threw a punch and caught the bastard in the cheek. Not the best spot to hit, and pain jolted up his arm, but he didn't care. He wanted to bring the fucker down.

His lion roared through him. Pressure built inside him and made his skin tight.

"Don't you fucking shift!" Trent snarled.

Power infused his words and choked off the push of his inner beast.

"Out," Trent ordered Rhys, then rounded on Dash. "You just had to push, didn't you?"

"Not my fault he's an asshole," he muttered.

"Load up your truck. You're on repair duty today."

"Can't play nice with others, won't play with anyone at all," Lindley added with a smirk.

Trent slashed a glare of warning in the second's direction. "Go," he growled, alpha power lacing a command into the words. "I want that fence fixed by the end of the day."

Dash bared his teeth in a silent snarl, spun around, and stalked out of the barn.

DASH DROVE the post hole digger into the ground. A savage jerk ripped it out again, leaving behind a gaping hole. Pausing to wipe his forehead, he glared down the line of broken posts. Only five more to discard and replace, then the wire work began.

Would have gone faster with extra hands.

Not that he had any regrets starting shit with the others. Assholes.

He stalked toward his truck and yanked out the new fence post. The order to repair the fence still buzzed in his head and chained his lion in place. The beast twisted and snarled inside him, ready to throw down with the others.

Dick sores. All of them. Gossipy, weeping, open dick sores.

His phone rattled in the cup holder of his truck where he'd left it. The stupid little merengue ringtone he'd assigned let him know the brother he didn't want was calling. Again.

"Motherfucker!" Dash roared at nothing, chucking the new fence post toward the pile of its mangled brethren.

The cattle in the nearby pasture barely even stirred. Dash glared in their direction. Inconsiderate heifers. Maybe he could stampede the whole herd through all the dens. He wouldn't even care if his got caught up in the destruction. Not like he'd be using it for long. Nothing left for him in Bearden.

The sound of hooves plodding along filtered through his frustration. He canted his head, ready to tell off whichever lion had come to check on him. He'd already been sent off like a toddler to timeout. He didn't need a babysitter to make sure he did his time.

After a second, his brows pulled together. The

noise didn't come from the Crowley side of the fence.

Dash spun his attention over the territory line.

Aw, shit.

The hooves he heard didn't belong to anyone in his pride, though he guessed that already. They didn't belong to anyone in the Ashford clan, either. As much as he would have loved to brawl with the bears, the rider heading for him was an even better treat.

But also, *fuck.*

He was a damn mess. Dirty and sweaty and hell, his shirt was torn. Was that blood?

Dash yanked the offending fabric over his head and wiped his face clean just as Colette reached the corner of the fence where he worked.

Her eyes met his, then roved down his body. The slow once over had his lion preening inside him.

Not a chance? Maybe that was the lie she told herself. The hungry interest in her look told a different story.

Maybe there was a reason to stay in Bearden, after all.

Dash lifted both arms and flexed like a body-builder. He showed off both biceps, then one at a time, ending with stretching his arms behind him and adding a coy wink over his shoulder.

Each pose dumped a little more amusement into her scent. Light, springy. Addictive. He wanted her laughs and smiles. He'd even take a roll of her eyes while she tried to keep both tightly bottled.

Colette hit the spot where she either had to pull her horse to a stop or barrel right into the fence. She twitched her mount's reins for a turn and kept on riding the fence line away from him.

"That's it?" he called after her. "Not even going to throw a dollar my way? I'm working this for you." He added an extra flex of his arms.

Colette glanced over her shoulder. Blue eyes sparkled back at him, but the rest of her face remained completely unimpressed as she turned her horse around to face him.

Her scent didn't lie. The cinnamon and forest notes thickened delightfully. Little bear was hot under the collar.

"You looked busy," she said in a bored voice. "I didn't want to distract you."

"I'd rather be getting busy with you." No joke, though he said it with a waggle of his eyebrows and a kiss on his flexed arm. No lie, either.

She barked a laugh, finally lowering her defenses

a fraction of an inch. That was all he needed to work his way in.

"I see you broke my brother's fence. Again."

"It was like this when I found it. I was just doing my neighborly duty by patching things up."

"Neighborly duty," she scoffed. "Trying to mend it before you got caught, you mean."

He tipped his fingers to the brim of an invisible hat. "Whatever the lady chooses to believe."

"Hm." She played with the reins while her horse cocked up a back foot and sighed heavily. "What time are you picking me up?"

Holy shit. Dash resisted the urge to rub a finger in his ear to make sure he'd heard her correctly. The expectant look as she waited for an answer was enough to know he hadn't imagined anything.

"I still need to repair this poor, spontaneously broken fence and fight the others for not helping," he said smoothly. "How does eight sound?"

"Maybe. What are the plans?"

"Dinner. Tonight."

She cocked her head, lips pursed. "Counteroffer. Quickie by the river."

Dash chuckled. "I won't say no to that, but you have to buy me a drink first. Man's got to have his principles."

"Fine," she agreed, smelling amused. "For your principles."

She didn't give him a chance to add anything else before whirling her horse around. "Don't be late!" she called over her shoulder.

Dash watched her until she disappeared on the other side of the hill, grin spreading from ear to ear.

Little bear wanted to run? His lion was more than ready to give chase.

CHAPTER 8

Colette sat on the edge of her bed. She drummed the fingers of one hand against the blankets while lighting up her phone to check the time with the other. She was dressed in jeans and tank top, with a button-down ready to be thrown on as she walked out the door. She'd donned her favorite pair of cowboy boots and even toyed with the curling iron to add some waves to her hair.

What the hell was she doing? Agreeing to a date? This wasn't how they worked.

Drinks, some scorchingly hot sex. That was her comfort zone. Anything else was danger and red flags and blaring sirens. She didn't want to get close to anyone. Especially not after the hell Jason put her through.

But the pained look that flashed over Dash's face that morning stuck with her. Worse than heartburn, close to a choking sensation, the fist-sized lump in her throat didn't disappear all through the morning and into the afternoon. The clawing and roaring of her bear ratcheted up until she could hardly pick out any other sound in the world.

She'd saddled up one of the ranch horses and raced across the snowy hills with the excuse of checking the fences for damages—a job Ethan shouted that didn't need doing—just to escape her own head. And fate, calculating bitch, put her right in the path of the painful temptation she'd wanted to avoid.

She still couldn't believe she'd prompted the ridiculous agreement for a date. Her only defense, as she saw it, was his shirtlessness. He'd whipped that thing over his head, and all those lines and stacks of muscles made her brain disappear.

Her bear gave a satisfied chuff that had Colette frowning at her phone. This was a mistake. She should call him and cancel.

Right on time, the low rumble of an engine reached her ears.

Butterflies took flight in her stomach before she stomped on the little buggers. She'd met up with

Dash loads of times. Just because he was picking her up didn't give her nerves free rein. Nothing was different about the night except for travel arrangements.

With a stubborn growl, she sat back down on her bed. Her bear pushed and prodded for her to get up and move, to get that man's scent in her lungs, to feel a laugh bubbling up from her middle over some dumb shit he said just to make her smile, but Colette didn't give in. She wouldn't have anyone—herself included—thinking she acted like a damn teenager waiting for her first phone call from a boy.

The truck pulled to a stop in front of the house. Metal creaked—the door opening, she figured. Then there was a brief moment of silence until hard knocks seemed to rattle the entire house.

She schooled her expression as heavy footsteps moved toward the door. Ethan, she guessed. Tansey moved through the house on lighter feet than the clomping bull steps her brother always took.

"Lion," her brother greeted in a less-than-pleasant tone.

"Bear," Dash answered, sounding bored. An edge of excitement entered his voice when he asked, "Colette around?"

"That's how you come here to collect my baby

sister?" Ethan dropped his voice mockingly. "'Colette around?'" His words returned to their normal range. "Is that what passes for politeness with you cats?"

"Ah, here comes the lion hatred." Colette could practically hear the eye roll in Dash's voice. "Lions planned the attacks. They want to kick all the other supes out of the enclaves. Go on. Let's hear it. I'm not a bear, so I shouldn't mix with your kind."

"It's not that you're a lion. It's that you're... you. Are we certain you even have a brain? Have you been scanned?"

"Who are you really insulting here? Because it was your sister's choice to come out with me."

Colette hopped to her feet and yanked open her door with a little more force than necessary. She hoped the extra noise would be enough to break up the squabble before it went too far.

"Hey," she greeted Dash with a bright smile as she hurried down the stairs.

Dash and Ethan faced off right in front of the door, with her not-date backed against it like he faced a firing squad. Only, the black look on her brother's face didn't seem to impress Dash in the slightest. Tansey lounged on one of the couches nearby, pretending to flip through an upside-down magazine.

Colette thought about going to her tiptoes and kissing Dash's cheek, but opted against needling Ethan too much, tempting though it was.

Dash peeled his eyes away from glaring at her brother. He brought his hand out from behind his back and shoved a bouquet of wildflowers at her. "These are for you."

Colette blinked before gingerly accepting the offering. "You bought me flowers?"

"Not exactly." Dash made a face and rubbed his hand over the back of his head. "The mates said this is what you do on dates, then raked me over the coals when I told them I didn't plan to bring you any. So really, they bought you flowers because I'm the biggest idiot in the world."

"You can say that again," Ethan muttered.

Colette jabbed her elbow into her brother's side. "Thanks," she said, at a loss for any other words.

She tried to ignore the roil in her gut and the sudden skittish need to flee. She didn't want flowers. Not from Dash. Not when the last man to buy any had been Jason.

Dash wasn't Jason, she reminded herself. He wasn't a threat.

Her brother stepped closer and eyed the bouquet critically. "They're a little wilted, aren't they?"

Dash slid a murderous look back to the man.

Balls. Time to go.

Colette shoved the flowers into Ethan's hand. She squeezed between the two men and reached for the doorknob, pushing Dash out in front of her. "Don't wait up," she tossed over her shoulder.

She was certain she heard a snarl and a snicker on the other side.

"Mighty fine family you got," Dash said as he cracked open the door for her.

Colette slid inside and shrugged. "They try their best. You're lucky it wasn't the entire clan. I heard Ethan complaining to Tansey he didn't have enough time to summon the troops."

He snorted, then closed her inside and jogged around the front to his door. Seconds later, he was behind the wheel and twisting the key in the ignition. "Ready? No sudden needs to attend? Makeup to apply? Bathroom break you didn't think to take before you left me breathing the same air as that bear?"

"Now that you mention it..."

A thicker air of concern replaced the light, springy teasing in his scent. "What's doing?"

Colette shook her head with a quiet laugh.

"Nothing! I'm joking. Let's get out of here before Ethan posts up with a rifle."

"Wouldn't be the first time he's taken a shot at me," Dash muttered. He threw his arm over the back of her seat and put the truck into reverse.

She fixed her elbow against the door and leaned her cheek against her fist. The house shrank down in the mirror as Dash raced down the ranch road. "And what did you do to deserve that?"

Dash glanced at her with pure innocence written in his eyes and a devilish smirk on his lips. "I might have—not admitting guilt, mind you—been involved in some minor vandalism to the old Ashford homestead."

"You used it as a scratching post, didn't you?"

"Might have. Again, not admitting guilt." Under his breath, he added, "That was just the first time."

Another laugh worked out of her before she could stop it and loosened the tight knot stuck in her chest. "He's not the only Ashford that knows how to shoot," she teased. "So you better not screw up tonight or there will be consequences."

Dash's eyes flooded with gold, and a smirk hitched up his lips. "That is not the threat you think it is, baby," he purred.

No. Warmth spread through her center. Definitely not a threat. But if the night went the way she hoped, neither would have any complaints.

CHAPTER 9

Colette eyed the restaurant, then gave Dash a flat look. "This is not what we agreed on."

Hogshead Joint looked packed to the gills. They'd circled the parking lot twice to find a spot way at the back and near the river. Lights strung around the deck railing and in the huge tree growing against the far side of the building made for a scenic little spot that felt far too romantic.

"We're still getting drinks," Dash assured, shrugging a shoulder. "There's just more involved now."

More involved. Like he hadn't left an entire meal out of the equation.

Unease sank in her stomach despite her best efforts to cast it away. The last time she'd gone out with a man cascaded into the worst years of her life.

Her bear snarled at the unwanted memories. Colette, too, let off an internal growl.

That was all behind her, now. Dash was at her side. He'd already made her laugh hard enough to make her cheeks hurt, and that was just the drive into town. She needed more of his complete disregard for propriety, definitely his hands on her body, and the escape both brought.

The night was about forgetting, and there was no better distraction than the rough, sexy lion that snagged her attention.

She continued lodging her fake complaint. "This was a trick. You're a dirty trickster."

Dash made a sound in the back of his throat. "While you're living the high life in the lap of luxury, I had to work all damn day. I'm starving. You can wait here in the truck if you want." He reached across the cab and scratched under her chin. "Like a good puppy."

Colette knocked his hand away with a laugh. "You're the worst, has anyone told you that?"

"Every damn day of my life. Sometimes more than once, if I'm lucky." With a final grin, he dropped out of his truck and hurried around the side to open her door.

She scrambled down before he offered her a

hand, though. She had her own principles to maintain.

Still, his words hit a sour note. "I'm not living the high life, you know. I've been forced back home when I'd rather be making my own way."

He slung his arm over her shoulder and started for the door. "You know, you haven't told me why. Does that have anything to do with your sudden turn to a life of crime?"

Flashes of memory pushed at her before she could stop them. She nearly stumbled under the weight of fear and sour despair. Damn it all to hell. She just wanted to be free.

Colette covered the sudden rush of unwanted emotions with an elbow to Dash's side. She jogged ahead a few steps before spinning to face him. "Come on. You'll have to do better than that."

His mouth hitched up in a lopsided smile. "You're making me work for it tonight?"

"Always. Where's the fun otherwise?"

He moved swiftly right as she reached the entrance, pressing her back against the door. Hand cupping her cheek, he skimmed his nose up the column of her neck. "Oh," he breathed against her ear, "we'll have fun."

Colette froze. A shiver worked down her spine as

she slowly lifted her eyes to meet his. Gold churned in the center of his hungry gaze. One breath filled her lungs with his scent and overwhelmed all her senses. Everywhere their bodies touched, heat flared to life.

He released her just as suddenly, backing away while swinging the door open. He scooped his hand through the air and ended in a short bow. "Ladies first."

"How chivalrous of you," she managed to say in a steady voice.

Dash locked eyes with her as she passed. Gold still churned with his normal grey, his mouth curved up in a devilish smirk, but he didn't say a word.

His hand landed on the small of her back and didn't leave until they were seated in a booth. By the time their drinks arrived and their dinner orders were placed, it became clear what drew the large crowd for a midweek explosion of business.

A trio of men took their spots under the extra strands of lights on the deck. Instruments were hoisted into position as the lead singer tapped his microphone. "One, two, one, two, three, four!"

The band launched into a fast-paced country song that had more than a few patrons mouthing along.

Colette shot Dash an exasperated look. "Band night?"

He settled an arm over the back of the booth and took a pull from his bottle. "There's dancing, too."

"Dash," she groaned.

He echoed, "Colette."

"Dirty tricks," she muttered.

He tapped her leg under the table with his foot. "Those are for later," he said with a teasing smirk.

Colette huffed a laugh and arched her brows. "Is there anything in this world you don't find fun?" she asked over the rim of her pint glass.

"Not really. Don't see the point in staying pissed all the time." His mouth twisted into an unabashed grin. "Flaring up and burning out, that's a different story. That's fun, too."

"Of course it is."

Their food arrived soon after. Plates piled high with ribs and pulled pork sandwiches made her mouth water as much as the smaller sides of artery-clogging deliciousness of hushpuppies, onion rings, baked beans, and mac and cheese. Colette dragged down a deep breath and exhaled with a smile. Food from Hogshead was one small bonus of being back in Bearden.

"Okay, tell me everything I've missed," she said to Dash, popping a hushpuppy into her mouth.

"Let's see…" He took a bite of his ribs and chewed thoughtfully. "Last time you were here, Trent and Hailey were trying to act like respectable citizens for her people, which ended with a shifter versus human fight with inflatable dicks tied around our waists. Shit, I gotta ask her where those went. I'd love to just place 'em randomly around to fuck with the others.

"Kyla showed up. Now Lindley isn't any fun, just like Trent. Which is dumb because Hailey and Kyla are some of the best people I know—present company excluded. And Rhys mopes around twenty hours out of the day for no damn reason."

"But there's more, isn't there? Your pride was in the middle of preventing the attacks on the SEA offices."

"We weren't trying to do anything. Lindley needed to get Kyla back. Everything else just happened." Dash shrugged and took another pull from his bottle. "Oh, did I tell you about the bullshit your brother is trying to pull with using our extra horses this year?"

Just like that, he turned the conversation away from anything heavy and back to wild stories.

Colette watched him for a long second before taking a sip of her beer.

Typical Dash. Nothing serious touched him for long. He downplayed the worst, highlighted the fun, and let everything roll off his shoulders. Even his characterization of a legitimately heroic action was distilled down to a few words. *Lindley needed to get Kyla back.* That was it. That was the goal. No embellishment, no justifications. They went in, did the job, and woke up to do chores the next day.

It was admirable, really. A change of pace from the braggarts at her last job. They'd so badly needed the attention that even the simplest tasks were played up as much as possible.

And in true, typical Dash fashion, he soon had her sides splitting in recounting the events she'd missed. From the uproar of the townsfolk waking up to find all the snowmen in the square with their carrot noses relocated to their waists and the subsequent search for the culprits to the pair of goats that terrorized the town for an entire day with their braying, head-butting ways, she was quickly filled in on the more eccentric qualities of the small town.

Dash cocked his head the moment they were done eating. "Dance with me."

No question. Not even a command, if she was

honest. A simple statement that expected only one conclusion.

"Dash," she groaned again.

Once again, he echoed, "Colette."

He stood quickly and offered her a hand. The second her palm slid into his, he yanked her to her feet. He spun her around to face him as soon as they reached the cramped dance floor. One hand landed on her waist while the other didn't let go of her hand. "I won't step on your toes. Promise."

That wasn't her fear. Getting close, giving in to the butterflies zipping around her stomach, those were scarier than having her toes crushed. She had rules for a reason. She didn't want to find herself at the losing end her father had experienced.

But, she had to admit, the night had been nice. The food was good, and the company kept her mind off her troubles. Her inner bear practically hummed with contented pleasure.

Dash spun her out, then drew her back into his embrace. The light caught in the eyes that never strayed from her, brightening to a burnished gold as they stroked up and down her body.

"I don't need flowers, you know," Colette told him softly. Heat sparked in her middle and spiraled through her with every twist and turn they took.

"That's what I told them." The hand at her waist moved to the small of her back, stroking slow circles. "Six-pack probably would have been a better idea."

"Now you're speaking my language." Colette tossed her hair over her shoulders, then wrapped her arms around his neck. The low purr that rattled in his throat made her pulse kick up a notch.

Over his shoulder, she thought she saw a flash of an unwelcome face.

Stiffening, she twisted to look around the restaurant. The hair on the back of her neck lifted. People —supernatural and pure human—talked and ate and drank. Despite the feeling of being watched, she didn't spot anyone looking her way.

No. He couldn't be in Bearden. He had to know what a horrible, awful, insane idea it was to follow her anywhere.

But it hadn't stopped him before.

She inhaled deeply, trying to pick apart the mess of scents from the crowded dance floor and packed tables. It was no use. Too many bodies moved and mingled until the jumble was unreadable.

Dash tightened his grasp. "You good?" he asked, brows drawing together. "You look like you've seen a ghost."

"Perfectly fine," she answered lightly. She shook off the spook and turned wide eyes on him. Before he put words to the questions written all over his face, she asked, "Want to get out of here?"

Dash's scent burst with hot anticipation that matched her own. Voice low, he rumbled, "I thought you'd never ask."

Colette stiffened when they burst back into the night. She dragged down one breath, then another, trying to find any danger. She came up empty again and again.

No Jason. He hadn't followed her.

Colette's shoulders slumped with anxious relief. She swallowed down the harsh laugh that wanted to bubble out of her. How? How the hell did he have such a powerful grip on her when she wanted nothing to do with him?

An arm fell over her shoulders and she jumped.

"Are you sure you're okay?" Dash asked.

The concern in his voice nearly toppled her over. Maybe it was the fun of the night. Maybe it was her idiot bear trying desperately to convince her to put her trust and faith in another person. Words sprang to the tip of her tongue, ready to be let loose.

And she froze.

What could he do that she hadn't already done?

He couldn't go back in time and warn her from ever agreeing to coffee in the first place. There was no stopping all the unwanted gifts and the barrage of phone calls. He couldn't prevent Jason from ripping through Myles Walsh's herd or her from jumping from her saddle to drive him off.

What was done, was done. She just wanted to forget and move on.

Colette turned into him, hands flattening against his chest, and leaned up to press a quick kiss to his lips. Heat flared in her middle and burned away the remaining worry gripping her heart. "All good," she said in a soft whisper. "What about dessert?"

Dash chuckled low in his throat as his hands threaded into her hair. His mouth crashed down on hers, devouring her from the moment their lips touched.

His tongue swept past her lips, twisting and tangling and daring her to meet him for more. He overwhelmed her senses, fried her brain, and she couldn't get enough. Couldn't ever get enough. He was the sweetest temptation in existence and the best distraction the world could provide.

This was what she wanted. She wanted to get lost in his touch. The feel of his lips was better than the hurts she'd taken. The quiet snarls and ragged breath pushed out the shouts and insults and threats of death. Dash was the cure to all her troubles.

They broke apart when the restaurant door swung open. The couple exiting gave them knowing looks before hurrying along on their way.

Dash pressed a kiss to her forehead and trailed his fingers down her frame until he reached her hand. "That's our cue," he rumbled thickly.

Colette nodded, then was spun around. He pulled her along, hand firmly locked with hers. The short journey was too long even for the arm's length between them; halfway to his truck, he tugged her closer. Arm going around her waist, he pressed himself against her back and pressed his lips to the crook of her neck.

Stumbling steps carried them the rest of the way. He pressed her hard against the side of his truck, hidden from prying eyes. "Fuck, Colette," he mouthed against her skin. "Can't wait to taste you."

Skies above, she loved the way his accent sounded. Thick and smooth, his voice stroked over her nerves. Heat seared through her, racing down her spine, until her skin felt tight and on fire.

One hand left her hair enough to rip open his door. Blindly reaching out, he shoved his seat back to make room, then dragged her into his lap.

"You did say you wanted a quickie by the river." His words ended somewhere between a dark chuckle and a growl.

Colette echoed his laugh, pressing her lips to his again. He swallowed the sound with another consuming kiss. Feverish desire gripped her. Need directed her movements. Quick fingers worked down her shirt, then shoved the halves off her shoulders.

The hand in her hair gently tugged her head to the side. His mouth went to her neck, licking and biting as his hands slipped underneath her tank top. "I missed this," he said, voice low. "Missed how you feel. Missed working you up."

He caressed her stomach, her waist, the small of her back. Heat roared through her at the excruciatingly slow path up her back, his thumbs coming dangerously close to the sides of her breasts before moving away again.

Heat pooled between her legs. Colette rolled her hips against him, groaning at his hard length trapped between them.

"Dash," she breathed. She rolled her hips again. So close, and they'd hardly undressed. "Need you."

"Mmm," he murmured against her neck. "I should take you home. Do this right. Make you mine."

Colette pulled back and eyed him sharply. Unease coiled tightly inside her. Words whispered through her head of other nights, another man. One she couldn't escape.

Her bear roared through her head even as a bucket of cold reality poured over her.

"What are you saying?" she asked carefully.

Dash lifted his eyes to her face. Grey and gold mixed in the center. "I want you to be my mate. My queen."

His voice rang with crystal clear honesty that rocked her to her core.

Her bear pushed and shoved and roared with an unholy desire to accept. No, need. Absolute, life-sustaining need that made her wobble where she sat.

"You feel it. I know you do," he said in the silence. He tugged her hand over his heart. "That beat is for you."

Sendings flashed from her bear. Hands running over slick skin. Lips following. Pure bliss written over both their expressions. Heat spread through her just from the images conjured by her inner beast.

Colette shoved them all aside. That future wasn't hers.

She didn't want a mate. There was too much risk involved. Life didn't hold any guarantees. Take her parents, for example. They were happy to start a family, grow their ranch, build up their clan. All their carefully laid plans meant nothing when their world crumbled into ashes.

Just like Jason threatened to do to hers.

No, that wasn't her future. Dash asked her for everything she couldn't give.

"I don't... I can't." She shook her head, the knife of panic pressing close to her throat.

"You can. We can." Dash lifted his hands from her thighs and cupped her cheeks. "It doesn't need to be now. Fuck, darlin', I've waited this long. I'll wait as long as you need."

The air thickened in her lungs. The sides of the truck pressed down on her. She felt trapped. Caged. Locked down and staring down the barrel of a life she didn't choose.

She didn't choose to come home.

She didn't choose to throw away a life outside the enclave because some crazy stalker manbaby couldn't accept her rejection.

She didn't choose to be born a shifter with instincts making demands of her.

Anger rose up inside her as she dug in her heels. Dash knew what she wanted. He'd played by the rules for years. And now he wanted to change them, on top of everything else in her life falling apart.

Her bear slashed at her insides. Sharp denials raked through her head. *Lies,* her bear seemed to roar. *Excuses.*

Colette closed her eyes against the rising pressure from her other half. The beast was at odds with her human side, wanting to give Dash everything he asked for while she wanted to run as far as she could in the opposite direction.

"Dash, you're not my mate," she said, more harshly than she intended.

Raw hurt flashed across his face before his expression closed off. In one swift move, he dumped her into her seat, then jammed a key into the ignition.

CHAPTER 10

The door of the Ashford home closed behind Colette with a thud not far off from a shot firing into the base of Dash's skull. His lion whipped through him, clawing, slashing, biting, tail twitching back and forth as the beast savaged him from the inside and demanded to be let out. He wanted to run as far and as fast as possible while still somehow busting down the door and walls that stood between him and his mate.

Dash bared his teeth in silent rebuke and spun out of the yard, not giving a flying fuck if anyone stood behind him. Idiot beast couldn't figure out his own desire.

Idiot man for thinking he stood a chance of taking a mate.

You're not my mate.

The words rang through his head, building louder and louder since they slipped out of her mouth. Hot bile roiled in his stomach, but there was no clearing out the sickness like he'd had a bad meal. His heart choked off his throat, lodged so firmly he could hardly draw breath.

He shouldn't have gotten attached. Not to Bearden, not to the Crowley pride. Not to Colette. Hell, he shouldn't have stayed in Bearden as long as he had. A couple months, enough to get him to the next town, that was all. He'd learned the ropes from his old man and kept playing the game long after he cut ties with the bastard.

Settling anywhere brought trouble. Better to not get attached to any one person, place, or thing. There was no telling when he'd have to leave it all behind in a mad, midnight sprint out the door, one step ahead of whoever had finally had enough of an Asher.

Staying in one place felt like drowning.

Leaving a place after getting attached felt like being ripped apart by the handful, only the ones doing it weren't nameless, stinking zombies. It was done by a gorgeous woman who smelled like the deep forests and cinnamon spirits.

You're not my mate.

He roared off Black Claw Ranch, screamed past the Crowley territory, and didn't stop until he slammed into a space at the warehouse used for shifter fights.

The smell of sweat and booze and excitement hung heavy in the air when he stepped through the open bay doors. The fighting ring that had sprung up outside of Bearden was nicer than most. Probably illegal six ways from Sunday, but the local Feds were a little busy forcing innocent supes to register for their future kill lists to do anything about a bit of drinking, gambling, and fighting. Plus, the people who ran the rings tended to handle any misbehavior swiftly and violently to discourage any copycats.

He'd seen their type all over the country. Run from them, too. They didn't like fixed fights or lions who tried to play in their gambling pool.

The crowd lining the bleachers cheered and stamped their feet for whatever action beat their fists inside the chain-link ring. Dash ignored it all as he shoved through the shifters mixing and mingling on the floor, swept past the bar constructed out of empty kegs and plywood over top, and elbowed his way to stand in front of the organizer.

Names and times were scrawled on a board

behind her. Flanking her sides were big, burly guards, and on their sides were the moneymakers— the bookies. Dash wasn't concerned with them. Win, lose, he didn't care. He just needed a fight.

Voice thick, accent heavy, he ground out between clenched teeth, "I want a slot."

The organizer's eyebrows rose up to her hairline as she eyed him sharply. "We're booked up tonight," she said flatly. "Try again tomorrow."

Fuck that. Fuck tomorrow. He didn't have until then. He needed a release. Needed to throw some blood and violence at his inner beast to soothe the hurts he'd taken.

Dash swiped a hand through the names chalked up on the board. The sharp cries of complaints registered as a dim buzz in the background. "There," he grunted. "Now you have room."

"Motherfucker—"

The organizer raised her hand to halt the guards coming for him. She exchanged glances with the bookies, then nodded and stepped aside. "Takes some balls to come in here like that." She eyed him up and down with interest. "You better put on a good show."

Another time, another life, he might have returned the look. Tossed her a smile. Maybe even told her to put her money on him and come collect later.

After Colette? Fuck, he'd hardly been able to look at another woman since she stormed into his life. Now that she'd ripped his heart from his chest, he doubted he'd ever recover.

"When?" he demanded.

The crowd broke into a loud roar and she slowly smiled. "Now, big guy."

He didn't wait to see who they lined up for him. Didn't care. His skin felt stretched tight over his frame; he needed to steady out the only way he knew how.

He ripped his shirt over his head as he neared the cage doors, then dumped out his pockets on the tiny table next to the man in charge of locking the fighters inside. Then he stepped inside the ring.

"Ladies and gentlemen," the organizer's voice rang out over the loudspeaker, "friends in fur! For years, you've watched him take down shifters bigger than him! And he's here tonight to bring you another round of bare-knuckled battery for the ages! Seeeeeeth Foster!"

Dash whipped around as his half-brother stepped into the ring.

The name tickled something in the back of his

head. Some undefeated record. He didn't know for sure and definitely hadn't seen the man fight before their first bout a week ago. The man hadn't had his own entrance announcement then, though.

Dash eyed him. "Get out of here," he warned.

"Why?" Seth asked. "Afraid of getting your ass kicked again?"

His lion snarled inside him. Dash's lips peeled back and made the sound a reality.

Even if Colette deemed him worthy of being a mate, he was a bad match. The evidence was right there, goading him into a fight. Waylon Asher strayed far and wide from his mate's bed. Seth was living proof.

The poison in Dash's veins already made his feet itch with the need to keep on walking and never stay in one place for too long. What the hell made him think he'd be able to stick to one woman?

He was an Asher, after all. Ashers were not mate material.

"This ain't for fun," Dash said in a low voice. He glanced over Seth's shoulder to the referee and cage manager. "Last chance."

Seth shot him an indulgent look. "Is that supposed to be frightening?"

The cage doors slammed shut; the rattle of the chain sealed off the only exit.

Dash shot forward, slamming his fist into Seth's face. The crack sent the man staggering back against the chain-link. He shook off the blow and blinked hard, then raised his hands to guard himself.

Fucker.

Dash lunged again. The second hit landed in Seth's middle, but his brother ducked the blow that aimed to take the nose from his face. Dash's arm swung through air where he should have come up against flesh.

He followed the move around in a circle. The light footwork kept him moving instead of stumbling into the pulled punch. He spun back around and kicked out hard, connecting his foot with Seth's middle.

The man wrapped both hands around his ankle. A savage twist took Dash down to the ground with a thud that left him momentarily dazed.

He rolled just before a fist slammed where his head had been, then shot back to his feet. Dash drove his knee into Seth's side and danced back before the man could grapple him. Close quarters were dangerous and hard to control.

"Gonna have to do better than that," Dash taunted. "Didn't anyone teach you anything?"

"Sure did," Seth panted. He jabbed out with quick punches, following Dash retreat across the ring. "Had the same teacher as you."

Dash snarled. So that was why Waylon never tried to get back his cash cow. He had another waiting in the wings.

His lion snarled through him. Dash shoved the beast aside. There wasn't enough time in the world to pick apart all the baggage Waylon left strewn through the world.

Seth sprang forward in a whirlwind of blows and a savage roar that the bloodthirsty crowd echoed. He caught Dash in the sides, the shoulders, broke through the arms he raised to protect his face. Dash crashed against the chain-link around the ring before he had a chance to claw his way back into the brawl.

He ducked Seth's next attack and let the man's knuckles meet hard metal. A sharp jab in the lower back kept him locked against the fencing until the ref whistled sharply and ordered them apart.

Dash pulled back, swaying from side to side, eyes bouncing over his brother to see what he'd do next.

What *Waylon* taught him to do next.

Asshole.

Seth feinted to the left, then swung a hard right.

Dash caught the punch, twisted around and laid Seth out flat. He planted a boot on the man's back and pulled on his wrist.

"Tap out," he snarled.

"Fuck you," Seth growled back.

Dash leaned back, boot holding Seth in place. The strain on his arm made him shake and groan, but he still didn't give up.

His lion roared and slashed inside him. The beast ached for the victory. Needed to see the man submit. The hard fight and final win was close at hand.

Sendings flashed through him. Blood on his muzzle. A bear at his side.

Dash yelled wordlessly to clear the images from his head. He yanked hard on Seth's arm, harder still, until the man writhed under his foot.

And pounded his fist against the floor.

Dash's lion roared with the victory, but the man felt nothing.

Chest heaving and feeling about a thousand times worse than before, Dash released Seth and stumbled back until he leaned against the chain-link. His face pounded with every beat of his heart and the way his chest hurt when he breathed, he'd be lucky if he only had bruised ribs.

Seth looked worse.

Face swollen, lip busted, probably a broken nose. He cradled his arm. Dislocated, maybe, definitely some stiff soreness in his future.

He knew he should feel guilty. The man hadn't done shit to him except be born from the same asshole that squirted him into existence. Even his rage had nothing to do with Waylon.

You're not my mate.

Nah, he was just a fuck up spawned by an even bigger fuck up.

His father hadn't kept a mate. He couldn't, either.

CHAPTER 11

"You came home early."

Colette dragged down a deep breath and kept marching across the great room and into the kitchen. Her grumpy glare took in the bouquet resting on the table which had magically multiplied overnight, then swept to her brother poring over one of the rifles usually locked in the gun safe.

Ethan lifted his head and added smoothly, "Do I need to kick some lion ass?"

He smelled positively thrilled over the idea. That, and the extreme care he put into cleaning the rifle threw a blanket of irritation over Colette thicker than the one she already wore. "That's some low-key sexism. Who says I can't do my own ass kicking?"

Ethan snorted. "No sexism. I'd do the same for

my sons." His eyes danced with teasing mischief when he raised them from his gun. "Gotta protect them from women like you."

Colette glared at her brother. "You're an ass."

"Yeah, yeah. You still love me."

"I'm reconsidering every remotely pleasant thought I've ever had about you," she said blithely as she poured herself a cup of coffee.

She shook her head when Tansey shook a box of cereal in her direction. Eating was out of the question when her stomach twisted and turned in greasy discomfort. Even coffee tested her limits, but she needed something to perk her up. That damned man had kept her wide awake all night without even being near her.

"And after all the nice things I've done for you. Take you in, feed you, not murder you in your sleep when you were teething and didn't stop crying for a week straight."

"If I cried for a week straight, when was I sleeping?" Colette licked the tip of her finger and marked a point on an invisible scoreboard at Ethan's grimace.

She took a seat at the table with him, angling herself away from the flowers. Which proved difficult without outright turning her back on them or shoving the vases further down the table. Leaves and colorful petals still tickled the edge of her vision and set her teeth on edge.

What the hell had he been thinking?

What the hell was she supposed to have said?

Her bear rumbled with displeasure and a dull throb began behind Colette's eyes. "Nothing happened," she gritted out.

Ethan's face broke into a grin of satisfaction. "Good. Very good."

Tansey swatted his arm. "That's enough out of you. Don't you have a ranch to run or something?"

Unaffected by his mate's scolding, he pushed to his feet. He shouldered the rifle, threw one last obnoxious grin over his shoulder, and strode for their bedroom.

Colette wished her narrowed eyes shot lasers when he started whistling a merry little tune. "Ass," she grumbled.

Tansey didn't correct her as she slid into the seat Ethan vacated. Her light brown eyes considered Colette with interest for a long second before she asked, "So what *did* happen last night? Because flowers left on the front porch can be very good or very bad."

Her heart lurched to her throat. She twisted in

her seat and eyed the second bouquet. Roses. Just like the ones Jason used to send her. "You mean those aren't from Ethan?"

Tansey shook her head and plucked a tiny envelope from somewhere in the middle. "Nope. They were addressed to you."

Colette kept her hands steady as she took the offered envelope. "You didn't read it, did you?"

Her brother's mate shook her head again. "But you better believe Ethan grumbled when I told him he couldn't snoop. I had to threaten him with mail fraud, which he said good luck proving and no one on the Bearden police force would prosecute, so I reminded him that the post office has their own people and they don't fuck around."

Colette forced a smile. The back and forth would have been sickeningly cute if she'd paid any attention, but the envelope captured her focus. Her bear paced through her with all the same anxiety her human half tried to keep in check.

The block letters that spelled out her name were all too familiar.

She ripped open the paper and drew out the note inside.

. . .

You've had your fun, but it's time to come home. I miss you. I need you. We belong together.

He didn't sign his name, but she knew exactly who'd left the flowers.

Her skin crawled with the violation. He'd been there, at her home. On her front porch. He'd waded through the territory thick with the scent of the Ashford clan, just to leave her a gift designed to make her afraid.

Worse, still, he'd probably been watching for a time to pull the stunt. Maybe he'd been in the crowd of Hogshead after all.

Colette jumped when a hand touched hers.

"Something wrong?" Tansey asked, concern lacing her tone.

She just wanted to rewind the clock to before she agreed to coffee with a stranger. Everything had gone wrong that night. She'd been harassed, outed, forced home, and had a mate dumped in her lap. She was exhausted from trying to hold everything together and act like her entire world hadn't spun out of control.

Skies above. Dash.

Jason probably saw Dash.

Just thinking his name broke a dam inside her. Longing flooded her veins. Guilt. Shock. Even the aches and pains turned up the pressure.

Her bear brushed fur against her mind with the silent demand to find the man and mend the break between them. When she didn't immediately stand and instead tried to pack those feelings away, the beast roared and clawed at her insides.

He knew the rules. She didn't want anything serious. Especially with threats leaving bouquets on her doorstep while she slept.

A mate bond was out of the question. She'd grown up a witness to the damage a snapped connection could do. Death was a mercy.

She couldn't count the number of times she'd found her father passed out at the table or the bleary looks he'd shoot her way when she'd tried to rouse him to take her to school. The house, the barn, the herd… everything had slowly fallen apart until Ethan grew big enough to tend the place himself.

The deterioration hadn't been just outward, either. The house had stunk with loss and desperation. Disappointment cut through often when he'd broken promises made while drunk, until she learned not to ask for anything. Her mother left behind a rotting hole in the middle of their lives.

How, how could she tie herself to that fate? Even if she wanted to believe she had a mate waiting for her, how did she hope to stop looking over her shoulder for the ruin no doubt barreling down on them? How did she survive if he took the brunt of Jason's insanity?

How did she sentence someone to that misery if she was the one to fall?

Almost every part of her disagreed. Too bad for her bear, her heart, and her body that her mind was still in control.

"Colette?"

She started. Tansey still looked at her expectantly.

She grimaced at the note still in her hand. The words seemed to laugh at her even when she crumpled the paper. She snatched the roses off the table and dumped them and Jason's threat forcefully into the trash.

The wildflowers stayed on the table.

"I have it handled," she said.

Tansey cocked her head and tapped a finger against her lips. "Ashfords," she said with a small shake of her head. Before Colette could retort, she added, "Would you like to come with us tonight? We'd planned for a mani and movie night, but I think getting out of the house might be best. Guests are due soon and there's no easy getting away once they arrive."

Out. She wanted out. Not just to the bar in the middle of town, not just surrounded by others who would be used to hurt her. She wanted a complete and total end to the trouble that trailed after her.

Holing herself up in her room would just bring more questions she didn't want to answer. Her brother's clan had their own lives. They didn't need to be bothered by an outsider's woes.

And she was an outsider.

CHAPTER 12

The trip to The Roost had been more fun than Colette expected. Drinks and bar food turned to rousing tales of Bearden and ranch life, and she found herself easing more into the group as the night wore on.

The women couldn't be more different if they tried. She'd even caught herself turning them into a joke several times through the night. *An innkeeper, a chef, a federal agent, a mad scientist, and a server walk into a bar...*

Still, they were all bound by one defining characteristic. They each had mates waiting for them at home.

Colette's bear pushed a sending on her that stole her breath. Dash, with a mate mark on his shoulder.

Her inner animal's pride was as difficult to ignore as the hurt in his scent was to forget.

The day had passed without a word from the man. Not that she deserved or expected to hear from him. No matter how much she lied to herself that everything was fine, she couldn't help feeling like she sat at a table while the world burned around her. The silence between her and Dash wasn't an invoking of the rules like when she left town. It felt heavier. Grittier. And all her fault.

Safer, too, she insisted. For them both.

"I am not a lightweight!" Joss declared with a slash of her finger through the air. Her unfocused eyes found her drink, and she smiled. "Oh, I have more!"

Colette shook herself out of her thoughts and turned her attention back to the group. The half-empty margarita apparently forgotten in the last thirty seconds determined Joss's words were a lie.

"You do not have more. That is mine," Tansey told her in an equally unsteady voice.

Colette grinned broadly as the two descended into good-natured squabbling over who the drink actually belonged to. With their attention fixed on each other, Liv dragged the margarita towards her and took a large sip.

"Finders keepers," she said quietly when she caught Colette's eye.

Colette turned a lock on her lips and threw the key over her shoulder. "Probably for the best."

She opened her mouth to say more, then snapped shut as her breath left her lungs in a rush.

Dash strode through the door, followed by the rest of his pride.

Colette's bear utterly swooned with delight the moment she inhaled the first faint thread of his scent. Baked earth, musk, fresh soap and cologne, the constant tinge of excitement, all the notes that went into making him warmed her from the inside out. Her mouth watered, her gums ached, and the bear shoved at her to *move.*

Shit. Balls. Shitballs. She didn't know what to do.

Talk to him? Apologize? Her bear stubbornly insisted she needed to get close to him and never leave his side, but she couldn't give him what he wanted.

No, she knew what she *needed* to do. Staying as far away as possible was the right move. The necessary move. The move that kept him out of the trouble that clung to her back like a thousand-pound gorilla. He didn't deserve the dark forces that stalked her from place to place, eating away at her life.

Eye fucking the hell out of him seemed a good compromise while she tried to reason her way into one action or another. Because tipsy Colette was still a total horndog for the sexy lion.

She glanced up again in time to catch his eyes pass over her. Recognition wasn't far behind. She tried to pull a smile, but froze when she saw him stiffen.

Her bear roared in pain and hatred for the entire living, breathing world. But mostly for Colette. *She* was the one keeping them apart from their mate.

Still, Colette pushed back on the beast. It was all too much. Her life was in shambles. She couldn't let her guard down. Not even to honestly acknowledge the hurt and pain and longing she felt when she was away from the man or the feeling of completeness she had when they were together.

Especially that.

Damn Jason. Damn his flowers and his obsession. Damn her father for not knowing how to handle loss and Ethan for somehow finding his way into the very same trap. Damn her instincts for trying to lure her there, too.

Colette felt like she stood on the outside watching through a door. The Colette on that side didn't worry about letting someone close and subsequently losing them.

She lingered on the edge, deeply afraid.

Afraid of letting go. Of losing control. Of getting what she wanted and having it blow up in her face.

Afraid she'd already screwed herself out of a chance at the mushy, gushy, frankly, stomach-turning, cuteness she saw in her brother and his mate and their entire clan. She'd spent so many years guarding against that very thing, she didn't even know how to begin to let someone in.

Only this wasn't some random person. This man was the one she kept returning to time and time again. He wasn't a bad guy. He hadn't deserved to be torn down because she couldn't handle her own thoughts and feelings and fears.

He made her laugh. And grin. And wreak havoc on the town. There wasn't a damn serious bone in his body—and she didn't care. She didn't want serious.

She wanted Dash and all his indecent irreverence.

Once again, she lingered in the doorway. This time, though, she didn't turn away.

She was an Ashford, dammit. Tough and mouthy, she didn't let a little fear stand in her way in every other part of her life. All the rules she put into place were designed to keep her from confronting her fear. Dash made her want to start breaking them.

Balls. No doubt about it, she was going to fuck up and burn the last standing structures of her life to the ground. If she hadn't done so already.

Grim determination filling her gut like a bag of cement, Colette flattened her hands against the table and prepared to push to her feet. She'd busted things between them. Fixing them was on her.

She glanced up and—

Oh, *hell* no.

Some woman had materialized by Dash's side. She laughed loudly at whatever he said, then leaned in close to rest her hand on his arm.

A possessive growl rattled in Colette's throat. Her blood pounded in her ears and her vision swam with red. Her bear surged to the front of her mind, ready to throw the female across the room.

"Colette?" Tansey asked, sitting up suddenly. "Everything okay?"

She barely heard the words as she stalked away from their table.

She tried to temper her inner animal. Really, she did. But the beast was high on instinct to fight and claim. Her fingertips tingled with the tips of claws and her gums ached with the press of her fangs.

Dash's eyes locked on hers from across the bar. He lifted his chin slightly, then with great deliberation, turned to the woman. "Order whatever you want," he said, eyes never leaving Colette.

She wedged herself between them without a care for the sharp, disgruntled squawk from the other woman. Bear riding her hard, she gritted out, "We need to talk."

His face stayed blank, but he stepped away from the bar. "After you," he said in a chilly tone.

Colette blinked, then took a quick glance around her. Every member of his pride purposefully looked everywhere but at her, the barfly shot daggers in her direction, and notice slowly rippled out from other groups. The privacy she wanted was nowhere to be found inside the bar.

She turned on her heel and marched for the door.

The cold night blasted against her skin the moment she stepped outside. Music and conversations thrummed and throbbed inside, but the stillness outside let her breathe and think.

And worry. And curse herself, her ancestors, and fate, but that was beside the point.

"Hey, Dash!"

Colette turned at the same time as Dash. A man raised his hand in greeting.

Dash let off a short growl, then turned away again, dragging her around the corner to give them more privacy.

"Who was that?" she asked.

"No one." He leaned against the wall, eyes swirling with gold as the silence pressed down on them both.

One second ticked by into another as she tried to account for what she'd just done. Acted like a fool, no doubt. A possessive, jealous...

Mate.

Holy hell. Her stomach dropped to her toes and kept on sinking straight to the center of the earth. Panic rose up in the hollow left behind, the same as she'd felt the night before when Dash told her flat out what he wanted.

What she'd already rejected.

What she couldn't—and absolutely wanted to —accept.

Dash folded his arms over his chest and canted his head. "You wanted to talk," he said sharply, "so talk."

Colette bit back the immediate need to deflect

and defend. She'd fucked up, and now it was time to eat crow.

Which meant letting her guard down.

"I… I'm…" Balls. Nothing seemed good enough. She was shit at getting close to people.

Dash looked at her expectantly. When she didn't continue, his mouth pressed into a hard line and his eyes darkened. "Right," he growled. "I'll leave you to it."

Claws slashed at her insides the moment he turned his back on her. Aches and pains washed over her, fisting her stomach, punching her right in the heart. Her lungs seized up as her bear threatened to steal control of her skin.

She wasn't ready for any of this, but she couldn't let the man walk away.

"Dash, wait!"

He turned, and she threw her arms around his neck and dragged him down into a hard kiss.

His surprise disappeared in less than a second. Colette gasped when his hands landed on her hips and spun her back against the wall.

Dash seized control in that second. He cupped her cheeks and tilted her head to slowly, teasingly, sip at her lips. The gentle press lit a match inside her and slowly raised her temperature until she felt like panting.

Then, and only then, did he deepen the kiss.

He let off a throaty, appreciative moan the moment he slipped his tongue between her lips. The sound dragged a hum of pleasure from her, as did the knuckles he brushed down her neck and over the swell of her breasts.

Electricity seemed to crackle between them, lifting the fine hairs up and down her body. But no, it was just him. All him. His scent, his touch, his entire presence surrounding her, overwhelming her, smoothing and stroking the same as the hands he ran up and down her body. Heat spiraled through her and left her needy and panting and wanting him. The hard length in his jeans that pressed against her said he was feeling the same.

Dash eased back before she combusted in his hands. He rubbed his cheek against hers, a purr rumbling in his throat. "So that's how it is?" he asked with smug satisfaction, accent thick as hell and stroking her in all the right places.

Colette shivered. Her heart pounded hard in her chest, the pulse matching the thrum deep in her core. The aches she'd felt all night turned brighter, hotter, and demanding of a relief only Dash could give.

She wanted to run.

She wanted to press herself against him until they tore each other's clothes off.

"Guess you'll have to find out." Colette untangled herself from his arms and stepped away, dragging her hand across his chest, over his shoulder, down his arm. His fingers closed on her wrist and squeezed before she took the final step away.

"No worries about that, darlin'," he murmured softly.

She didn't turn. Turning meant letting him have the final word. She was willing to give this… thing a shot, but she couldn't make it too easy on him.

Still, her cheeks burned and her stomach dipped in wild anticipation.

CHAPTER 13

"Hey, pretty lady," Dash murmured quietly. Some of the cows looked up at his voice, but most held their ground, unwilling to give up on their rest until he brought out the tasty stuff. The one nearest the fence, all black except for her white face and a splotch on her back, leaned heavily into the hand he rested against her swollen side.

No calves, but that was fine. They were still weeks out from the proper start of the calving season. Didn't stop him and the others from checking every day in case one came early and needed extra care.

"But you'll be the first, won't you, pretty lady?" he murmured with another long scratch. "Gonna make us all that prize money?"

Each year, the ranchers in the area threw in some cash as an entrance fee for the Calving Celebration. The whole thing was just one of the many ridiculous and unnecessary shindigs Bearden put together. He wasn't one to judge the need for a good party, but call a spade a spade. The first calf to hit the ground on spindly legs was simply an excuse to get wild, no matter what anyone told him about traditions.

Still, the first ranch to show off their new addition took home all the prize money. Trent split the cash with the rest of them for a nice bonus when they won, but the real treat was getting one over on their biggest rival, the Ashfords.

Though, with that flip Colette pulled on him, maybe he should make nice with the bears. Their alpha was her brother, after all.

Dash made a face. Yeah, right. When hell froze over.

His scowl turned to a wide grin as his lion stretched through him with a gentle kneading of his claws. The beast nearly vibrated with the purr that rocked in and out of his chest. Sendings flashed, hot scenes balanced with picture-perfect domesticity. Every last one of them gave a glimpse of a mate mark on Colette's skin.

Something had changed her mind, and he was

damn sure it wasn't pure instinct of seeing someone approach him, though the color that flashed to her eyes had been hot as hell. Not that he'd tell her. Or at least, not so soon. His pretty little bear couldn't be pushed too far without snapping up her walls and locking him out. He had to hunt her patiently. Slowly. Chase her so delicately she didn't know she was caught until she couldn't breathe without him.

He'd waited years already. A little longer wouldn't hurt.

He gave the cow a final pat, then slipped through the fence. Night hadn't been quite cold enough for a freeze, but he knew Trent would make them check the troughs until the last of the snow finally melted.

By the time he finished the circuit, the crunch of tires reached his ears. He trudged back toward the barn and the inner paddock while three trucks pulled to a stop.

"What the hell are you doing out here so early?" Lindley called out to him as he exited his truck.

Dash raised his middle fingers. "Working. Where have you lazy fuckers been?"

Another side effect of Colette giving him the time of day—he didn't feel the need to run. The itch that had coursed through his entire body, throbbing opposite to the beats of his heart, ended the moment she threw herself into his arms.

She was a damn miracle worker, that was for sure. He needed to make himself worthy of her salvation.

He'd already done the first step by showing up for work before the others. That was serious, responsible bullshit. Better, even, than the mated males in the pride. Trent and Lindley routinely found themselves enticed into lateness by the feminine wiles of their mates.

His lion rolled through him again before Dash shoved the beast to the back of his mind. Mate material. He needed to prove himself mate material before he claimed his mate. Then he could have late mornings until the end of his days.

"Guess that talk with Colette went well," Rhys said.

"Because the grin he wore all night wasn't a dead giveaway?" Trent grumbled, then fixed him with a hard look. "You were supposed to stay away from her."

Dash shrugged unapologetically. The tensions between Trent and Ethan weren't his concern. If anything, Trent should be thankful. Fucking with the bears was practically a job description. He'd just taken it to a whole different level.

He kept his damn mouth shut, though. Mate material, he reminded himself. He couldn't go starting brawls for no reason.

"When has he ever listened?" Rhys added.

Dash narrowed his eyes at the other man. He couldn't start brawls, no. Finish them? Different story altogether, and Rhys looked like he wanted a fight. Tight shoulders, clenched jaw. The scarred lion only needed to flash some silver into the man's eyes to complete the about-to-snap picture.

Who was he to deny the beast what he needed? His lion sat up inside him and licked his lips in anticipation.

Dash jabbed a finger in Rhys's direction. "You're a nosy motherfucker. Anyone ever tell you that?"

Rhys lifted a lip in a silent snarl, but Lindley jumped in before he could say a damn word.

"Someone has to keep an eye on you. Who knows what trouble you'll pull down on our heads," Lindley snarked.

"Aw, Lin, you still grumpy over the bar fight the other night?" Dash grinned and leaned against the wood slats of the paddock fence. "You know how it goes. You chomp my leg to bits, you gotta have my back in a brawl. Fair's fair."

A brief flash of guilt passed across Lindley's face. Dash frowned. Shit. He hadn't meant to make the guy feel bad. Sure, he'd walked with a limp for a couple weeks after playing chew toy to a lion hell-bent on murdering his way through his father's pride, but he was healed up. Mostly. A little extra stiffness in the morning didn't count for anything weighed against the shitshow that night could have been. They'd pulled Lindley off a suicide mission, saved Kyla, set the baddies up for a life behind bars, and made their way home. Nothing to it.

"Unless…" Dash taunted to take the sting out of the air. "Unless you're not up for a tussle? Maybe you can't handle a little human swattin' at you? We all know Hailey snipped the boss man's bits; is Kyla carrying your balls in her purse, too?"

"You little shit," Lindley growled. He snapped forward, arm wrapping around Dash's neck.

The fence between them kept the blows light, but Dash wouldn't have cared even if Lindley let loose. He'd rather burn off a little aggression than let the man stew in unneeded guilt all damn day.

"Ease up, ease up," Trent griped. When the scuffle broke apart, he leaned against the fence. "We need to talk about the upcoming season. We've been short a hand since that fucker Garrett turned traitor."

Dash let off a growl. The others, too, rumbled with displeasure. Fucker was too generous of a description. Weak-willed nut weasel. Yellow-bellied goat licker. Shitstained, shit-for-brains, asshole. Bad enough the bastard handed Hailey over to Trent's batshit uncle with a hard-on for killing all humans. Garrett's career as an ultimate sleaze ball took him to running women for the consortium of lion prides beholden to Jasper himself. He'd been there when shit hit the fan for the consortium ranks, but escaped before any of them could rip his head from his body.

Fucker.

Huh. The word did fit pretty well.

Trent fixed them all with a warning glare. Gold swirled in his eyes and the air thickened around him with the pressure of his inner lion demanding their attention. "I put out the word around town and surprisingly got a hit before needing to look afield. Lion by the name of Seth Foster."

Dash jerked upright. "Who?"

Trent lowered his brows. "Seth Foster. You know him?"

"Just through the fight nights," Dash answered hastily.

Not a lie. Not exactly. Just a very slight omission of information.

Trent shrugged and continued, "Doesn't have much experience in ranch work, but says he's looking to settle around here. I'd rather train someone up who's looking to stay than get someone in and lose them at the end of the season."

Well, color him stalked.

Dash didn't know whether to be offended or flattered. Offended because, well, duh. *Half*-brother dear wasn't exactly a welcome sight. He also had an annoying similarity to the rest of his dumbfuck pride with inserting himself where he didn't belong.

On the other hand, the *brother* portion of that half-brother combo was growing on him. He'd relied on himself for a long while and learned that blood didn't mean shit when the hard times rolled up. Family, on the other hand, stuck together no matter what crisis threatened to break over their heads.

Dash took the Crowley pride in with a sneaky glance. They'd loaded up to hunt down Garrett when he stole Hailey, then joined Trent in the battle to kill the shit out of his limp-dicked uncle. When Lindley lost his head and nearly lost Kyla, they'd been there to rip through assholes trying to keep the two apart. Hell, they even took turns playing mouse to Rhys's kitty cat when the man's inner beast snatched control and needed to bleed something.

They were closer to a family than his own flesh and blood, though he'd need a night of hard drinking to admit it out loud.

But maybe, just maybe, his mystery relation wouldn't be an utter disappointment like the rest of the Asher males. Himself included.

"Where is he going to stay?" Lindley frowned. "Sage has been living in the cabin Garrett vacated."

"She could move into my den," Rhys said in a low rumble.

Lindley shot the man a dark look that made Dash take a step back, and he wasn't even the target. Trent wanted to keep him apart from Colette to avoid any trouble? Good luck avoiding the bomb slowly ticking toward an explosion in their midst.

"No one is moving anywhere," Trent growled in irritation. He lifted his eyes to the sky, then scrubbed a hand down his face. "We have the extra room in the barn. Storage will be a little tight everywhere else once it gets cleared out, but half the junk in there needs to be thrown out anyway. This is as good a reason as any."

"Sounds like Rhys already volunteered. If he's so willing to move Sage, he can move for Seth." Dash grinned. "Hey, they're close enough names. Four letters, starting with S…"

"Shit," Rhys said slowly, "no."

Trent ran a hand down his face. "We will all pitch in—"

"Just Rhys the most," Dash finished.

The other man whipped a punch in his direction.

Dash danced back, urging Rhys on with a tilt of his head and crooked fingers. "Come on, big guy. Not such a tough kitty, are ya? How're you gonna carry all them boxes?"

Rhys snarled, eyes flashing to silver in the time it took to blink. He lunged for Dash.

Hell yes. This was what he lived for. A good fight, hard breath in his lungs, heart racing.

Fists collided with his sides. He laughed as he jumped out of range, luring Rhys into motion. As soon as the other lion shambled forward, he bolted behind and nailed him in the back.

Rhys spun around, snarl on his lips. His eyes flashed even brighter right before his lion ripped out of his skin. The white beast let off a savage roar, then threw himself toward Dash.

"Motherfucker!"

His own lion burst out of him, meeting the charge with a savage swipe of a paw against Rhys's face. It did nothing to stop him. He slammed into Dash, taking him down with a hard shoulder to the chest.

"Son of a bitch," Trent growled. "Change back! Now!"

Like hell he would. He'd gotten an early start to his day. He could win a brawl before getting back down to business.

He was trying to make himself mate material, not a fuckin' angel.

CHAPTER 14

Colette paced in a slow circle while she waited for her ride to show.

Oh, who the hell was she kidding? *Her ride?* Dash. She waited for Dash. All six feet and extra inches of living, breathing, laughing, fighting lion who twisted her up until she didn't know which way to turn.

Her bear chuffed eagerly for the man to arrive and, once again, Colette didn't know how to handle the butterflies that detonated a mega fuckton question bomb in her stomach with every damn flap of their wings.

What the hell was she doing?

Getting possessive over a man wasn't like her in the slightest. Love 'em, leave 'em, forget their names the next day was the uncomplicated way to live.

Anything else asked for all those emotions she'd pushed to the dark spaces of her mind and marked off with bright yellow police tape to warn away unauthorized crossings.

Getting close to anyone *hurt.* Getting close was dangerous.

But she'd felt the world fall out from under her feet several times in the space of just a few days and she was tired of feeling like she lived on the outside. Dash always made her feel part of the moment when they were together. Didn't matter if they were drinking or joking, he held both woman and bear in his thrall.

Plus, she still needed to apologize. They'd kissed, they'd agreed to a do-over, but she still hadn't said sorry for shoving him away when his only crime was rightly calling her out on feeling something for him.

Yep, that was as solid of a rationalization as any.

Colette leaned against the railing and wrapped her arms around herself to better hold her bear in control. The beast danced and bounded through her with the elegance of a… well, a bear in a frilly pink tutu. Given the chance, she'd ignore all of Colette's deeply ingrained caution and let the man mark her without a care or question.

The door whipped open and Ethan strolled into

the night with the casual air of someone on a mission. Without a glance at her, he took a seat on one of the benches, then leaned forward and began sharpening a long, deadly looking knife.

Colette stopped in front of him, folded her arms over her chest, and glared. "What are you doing?"

Ethan slowly lifted his head from his work. Pure innocence sparkled in his eyes. "Me? Oh, just doing a little chore I've been putting off."

"I wanted to avoid this. That's why I came out here. Alone."

"Well, you see," he started lightly, restarting the sharpening, "you can want in one hand and shit in the other, then tell me which fills up the fastest."

Colette rolled her eyes and strode away from him. "Skies above, I hope someone challenges you for alpha and wins."

Ethan chuckled. "And yet, no one will step up. Probably because they know they'd have to deal with you and Tansey afterward."

She opened her mouth to tell him to get back inside or *she'd* challenge him—and win—when the sound of a truck roaring up the road cut her off. The miserable growl that rattled in her brother's throat made her grin from ear to ear.

Colette was down the steps and to Dash's truck before he even cracked open his door.

"You better get her home at a decent hour!" Ethan called.

Colette rolled her eyes as she hauled herself into the cab. "Yes, *Dad.* We'll be sure to ignore all your requests."

"Hey," Dash rumbled at her side.

Colette slammed the door on Ethan and turned to face the other man. His mouth hitched up in a lopsided, sexy smile that sparked an ember of warmth in her middle. Her bear settled down with a sigh of contentment, wrapped snugly in a blanket of his baked earth and spiced scent.

"Hey," she answered. Incredibly casually, of course. She wasn't some besotted bear.

Her inner animal growled in denial.

Thankfully, Dash broke their look and started them on the road into town.

She fidgeted in place as the seconds ticked into minutes. The air weighed down on her. Or maybe in her; her lungs filled with his delicious, musky scent. Colette swallowed hard and willed her heart to stop tripping in her chest.

What the hell was she doing?

She wanted to throw herself out of the truck. She wanted him to pull over and put those fingers so tightly wrapped around the steering wheel to work. And all the while, her bear romped through her head.

"Any new brawls today?" she asked, fighting to keep the strangled quaver out of her voice.

"Mmm," Dash hummed. "Not a complete day without one. It's a bonding experience."

She huffed a laugh and lost a fraction of the nerves she didn't want to admit existed. They were on their way out together, but he was still just… Dash. "And what, pray tell, were you bonding over today?"

"Trent has this dumb shit idea of bringing on another hand so we're prepared to kick your brother's ass during calving season." He turned to her and waggled his eyebrows. "I know a job if you're looking."

"Pass. Hard pass. I was raised in dysfunction and you lions," she swirled her finger in the air at him, "need years of therapy to sort out your issues."

"I'm not paying some head doctor to tell me what a few drinks and a fistfight will sort out. Kiss your job offer goodbye," he scoffed. "I'm going to let Trent hire my brother."

Colette twisted in her seat to better take him in. "Wait, brother?"

He canted his head to the side in acknowledgment. "I shouldn't be surprised. My old man took 'be fruitful and multiply' to heart, apparently. He kept his other women hidden for the longest time, even while we were on the road for fights, but it wrecked my mother when she found out. Wouldn't surprise me if there were more Seths out there. Asshole."

Huh. After all the years they'd known each other, he still managed to surprise her.

Then again, when they spent most of their time joking or getting naked, there wasn't a whole lot of exchange happening regarding the state of the world, their families, or their innermost desires. Hence the shock and surprise when he laid his cards on the table.

In a way, she felt like they were starting over completely. She wanted to peel back all his layers and see what was underneath.

By the time he hooked a turn into the parking lot of The Roost, her nerves had all but disappeared. Her whole body seemed to buzz with relaxed excitement.

Colette jerked a thumb across the street. "No food?"

"Aw, nah. I tried that last time. Learned my lesson, too." He winked. "I watched a couple highly informative movies on the subject."

She snorted. "Porn does not count as instructional material."

"I was not talking about porn. And we'll have to agree to disagree on the instructional value." Dash reached into his pocket and drew out a slip of paper. He carefully unfolded it, slid her a significant look, then cleared his throat. "'Do not expose to direct sunlight.' I've seen you out and about, so I think we're safe there. 'Do not get wet.'"

Colette snickered as she dropped out of the truck. "Oh, that's been broken."

His mouth twitched, but he didn't take the bait. "'Do not feed after midnight.' Now, we're still a few hours away, but I think this is the rule we really need to pay attention to."

"I am not a gremlin."

"Again, agree to disagree—ow!" Dash danced away with a laugh after her elbow found his side. He caught her in a tight embrace, arms pinned to her sides, and rested his chin on her shoulder as they continued toward the bar. "Maybe we can make an exception this once."

"How magnanimous of you," she said dryly.

He chuckled and reached for the door over her shoulder. Noise washed over them as they stepped inside. Dash scanned the crowd, then leaned close. "Why don't you grab us a table and I'll elbow up to the bar for drinks."

Colette nodded. Dash's hand dropped to her hip and gave her a squeeze as she started to step away. His fingers dragged along her lower back until they finally parted.

She resisted the urge to close the distance again.

Weaving through the other patrons, she stole into an emptying table before anyone else could snag the seats, then glanced toward the bar. True to his word, Dash elbowed aside others until he was front and center... and ignored. Gideon and Leah pointedly looked over his shoulders to the customers he'd jumped ahead, much to Dash's frustration.

"Hey, sugar."

Colette whipped around to find Jason settling into the seat reserved for Dash.

Her bear rose to her feet inside her, ready to swipe heavy paws against the wolf and drive him away. Away from her, away from the herd of cattle he'd savaged, away from the entire freaking enclave. He didn't belong in Bearden. She'd had assurances he wouldn't bother her again.

Yet there he was, looking at her with the same sad eyes he'd flashed at her when she told him she wanted nothing to do with him.

"What the fuck are you doing here?" she breathed.

Her initial shock fading, she took a better look at the man. Dark hair, dark eyes. His whip-thin body was corded and packed with hidden power at the best of times, but he looked off right then. Sick, even. Like he hadn't slept or eaten for days.

A shudder ran down her spine and her bear watched with caution. Jason wasn't a man to underestimate. She'd made that mistake, then had to watch him systematically dismantle any safety and security she possessed.

Seeing him brought back all the horror and death she wanted to forget.

"I'm here for you. Where else would I go?"

"For me?" she sputtered. "You're here for me? Skies above, you should be as far from me as possible after what you did."

Jason shrugged. "So I made some mistakes "

"Mistakes?" Colette growled low in her throat. She planted her hands on the table and leaned in close to keep from shouting at him. "Your mistakes cost me a job. I have to register because of you!"

"We're going to take care of that, sugar. Don't worry. We're going to get back at that asshat Myles Walsh for what he did to you."

"We—" Colette shook her head. "We're not doing anything. There is no 'we'. I want you to leave me alone."

Jason reached across the table and dropped his hand over hers. Big, sad eyes found hers. "You protected me, sugar. I know what that means."

Oily, slick slime coated the back of her hand and oozed up her arm. Or, at least, that was how it felt to be touched by the man seated across from her. No warmth, no butterflies, nothing pleasant. He made her skin crawl.

"It means nothing." She tried to move her hand, but he grabbed hold and refused to let go.

"I waited for you," he said in a harder voice. "I waited, but others bailed you out and took you away."

She barked an incredulous laugh and tugged harder. A thread of worry wove through her when she couldn't break free. "Why the hell would I go anywhere with you?"

Jason's eyes widened like she'd spouted off the same sort of nonsense that ran out of his mouth.

"Because you belong to me. No one will keep us apart."

Hell no. Hell fucking no.

She didn't belong to him. She didn't *belong* to anyone. Her life was her own. She was a grown woman capable of making her own decisions. And she'd decided five minutes into a single outing with Jason that she absolutely didn't want to get to know him better.

Colette growled again, her bear stretching her skin tight. "Myles isn't to blame. You are. I don't know how you gave your alpha the slip, but you need to go back to your pack. Own your shit, Jason."

"My alpha," his lip curled in disgust, hand tightening around hers, "tried to keep me from my mate. So I took his head and his pack."

Holy shit.

Every cell in her body revolted at being so close to him. He'd gone beyond obsessed and into the realm of totally deranged.

"Who's this?" Dash asked.

Colette sat back quickly and yanked her hand out from under Jason's. "No one," she said hastily. She hated the pang of guilt that jolted through her. "He was just leaving."

She slid a look from Jason to Dash. Gold eyes

flashed as the two stared at one another. The air thickened with aggression, both men one snarl away from lunging over the table.

But only one casually confessed to murder.

Balls. She needed to get them apart before Jason tried to add another body to his kill count.

Pain and panic wrapped around her heart at the suggestion of a world without Dash. Her bear whipped through her, a destructive force hell-bent on keeping their mate safe. She was ready to fight off a thousand wolves to keep their future alive.

"I'm not going anywhere without you," Jason growled.

Damn it all to hell.

Colette jumped out of her seat to stop the brawl before it began. She planted her hand on Dash's chest. Warmth flared against her palm and cut the sinking feeling in her gut. "Let's go."

A snarl left Jason's lips and dragged the lion's attention back to the other man.

All her caution zipped back into place. She didn't want Jason staking a claim on her. She didn't need Dash going all hotheaded brawler on the man. And she sure as hell didn't want to suffer more loss.

By the Broken, why couldn't he have just left her the hell alone?

Colette growled to herself, unsure if she meant Jason or Dash.

She pushed Dash, then pushed him again when he didn't stop glaring at Jason. He finally broke on the third shove when she slipped around him and made for the door.

Her heart jumped into her throat and she felt too hot, even in the chill of the night. She wanted to run. Far and fast and away from Jason. Away from Dash, too. Away from anyone Jason would hurt to get to her.

"Who was that, Colette?"

She didn't turn around to answer. "It's none of your concern. I can take care of myself."

Like she'd taken care of herself when Jason first turned into a problem? Or when he'd tracked her down and destroyed her career? Or when he overthrew his alpha and followed her home for more torment?

"Not my concern? Not my—" Dash cut off a curse, then jogged after her. Grabbing her arm, he spun her around to face him. "It sure as hell *is* my concern when you smell pissed off and scared and have some asshole bothering you."

"You think so?" She arched her brows and eyed him critically. "Then I guess you'd better be concerned with yourself right now."

He met her look without backing down an inch. "Whatever you're running from, you don't have to do it alone."

He was wrong. He was so, so wrong.

Over his shoulder, Jason pushed out into the night. He stood, staring, eyes glowing in sharp contrast to the darkness around him. Every inch screamed fury.

His wolf ripped out of him and he disappeared into the darkness.

CHAPTER 15

Dash once again watched the door of the Ashford house slam shut with him on the other side. Shadows moved against the windows of the great room before one turned away and moved out of sight.

He counted the seconds it'd take to move up the stairs, then down the hall. He trailed after Colette in his head.

What the fuck had happened?

She'd given him no explanations. No words at all, even. From the moment she loaded into his truck, it was like she'd disappeared completely. Her body occupied the same physical space as his, but he doubted she'd heard any of his attempts to draw her into conversation. She'd retreated back behind her walls and into a mile-high tower surrounded by crocodiles.

His lion roared through his head. Claws slashed at his insides. Fangs pressed against his gums. Sendings flashed like someone had hit the fast-forward button of a murder spree. Red, so much red, with that asshole from the bar torn to pieces in the middle of the bloody storm.

No one touched his mate. No one made her smell of fear and fury.

Fuck, he'd been so worried when he turned to find her at a table with someone else. His blood had pounded in his ears when that man reached for her hand. They'd looked awfully cozy together from his spot across the bar.

And then he'd lurched to a stop and heard her pulse racing. That'd been enough for his lion. The other shifter had to go.

Except she'd stopped him and hightailed it out of the bar like her hair was on fire.

Dash eyed the front door. He wanted to bang it down and demand answers, but he knew it was the wrong move. There was no talking to her when she was locked up tight. Pushing for more wouldn't tickle any answers out of her. She'd probably stab him if he kept trying.

She needed time. Space. Things that went against his every instinct to stick by her side and protect her from any and all threats. How the fuck could he be her mate if she wouldn't let him in?

Ethan yanked open the door and glared into the night. Dash knew better than to try to muscle his way past the alpha bear, even if he stood between him and his mate. She needed time to cool off, and he needed time to figure out how to sneak past her defenses.

Dash lifted his fingers from his steering wheel in a halfhearted greeting, then tore off the ranch.

His lion fought him every rotation of his wheels.

He glared at the road leading to his den, then kept on driving. Last thing he wanted was Trent giving him the told-you-so lecture or worse, those big cow eyes filled with pity because his damn mate wanted nothing to do with him.

A fight was off the table, too. His lion ripped claws through his middle and roared in his head. Not loud enough. He could still hear the damn silence from Colette.

No, no fights. Not until he had a fingernail of control. He didn't need a body on his conscience. Besides, if trying to get through Colette's invisible walls proved difficult now, he didn't want to know the trouble he'd face with the actual walls of a prison between them.

He sure as shit wasn't going back into Bearden. Not without a kill order, anyway, and with Colette locked up tighter than Fort Knox, he wasn't liable to get any answers.

Dash scrubbed a hand down his face. Defiant Dog was his saving grace. He planned to drown himself in booze until he could think straight.

He walked through the doors of the small, grimy bar on the edge of enclave territory, and then almost walked out again. His half-brother sat in a corner with another man Dash didn't recognize. Didn't want to know, either. Nope, not interested in anything involving another of Waylon Asher's sons.

He gritted his teeth because fuck if he was driven off for the second time that night. With a warning glare to leave him the fuck alone, Dash sidled up to the bar. "Two bottles of beer," he growled to Hector.

He downed the first as soon as it appeared, fingers tightening around the neck. He wanted to throw it. Shatter the glass. Maybe even pick up a broken piece and make damn sure that fucker who had Colette smelling so scared and angry never bothered her again.

He flicked the bottle closer to Hector's side of things and nursed his second drink.

Fuck, he felt stuck. Any other time, he'd bolt. Find a new place to make a few bucks, kill off the thinking parts of himself with booze and brawls. This was different. His mate was on the line, but he didn't know how to keep her.

Seth slid into the seat next to him.

Not the time. Not the fucking time.

Dash pointed at the man with his bottle. "You're nosing in where you're not wanted. Coming to *my* bar, taking a job with *my* pride."

Stalker. Brotherly, slightly endearing stalker, but stalker nonetheless. A little impressive, too. It wasn't every day a mystery relative appeared and agreed to learn an entirely new skill set just to spend some time together.

Dash snorted. Maybe they were more alike than he cared to admit. Relentless pursuit seemed to be a trait they shared. He chased after Colette, Seth chased after him. Time would tell if either got what they wanted.

Seth shrugged, then raised his fingers to summon Hector. A shot of whiskey and a beer appeared a few seconds after ordering. He tapped the shot glass against the bar, then tossed back the alcohol. "You killed my streak," he muttered, staring straight ahead. "You take from me, I take from you."

Dash cocked his head at the other man before the words sank in. Then he spun around and sipped his beer. "Guess you're just not as good as you thought," he stated blandly.

"Name the night. Best two out of three." His brother's lips twitched with the hint of a smile. Then he sobered, his scent turning cold and aloof. He unfolded his wallet and pulled an envelope from inside. "I don't know how else to do this, you won't take my calls, so I'm ripping off the bandage. Waylon's dead. He left this for you."

Dash stared at the envelope like it was a snake coiled and ready to strike. Raw anger burned in his gut. Shock, too. He hadn't laid eyes on the man in years, had all but expected the news, but the blow was still the same.

His father was dead.

The words sounded strange in his head. His lion swiped a paw to clear them. There was no changing the fact that his father was dead.

Asshole. He hadn't deserved the woman he claimed as a mate. None of the people he touched had deserved the poison he left behind.

Dash turned narrowed eyes on Seth. "That's where you've been all this time? At his sickbed?"

Seth raised his hands, face stony. "No, I didn't keep this from you. I had other business and found out at the tail end of things. He was dead and burned a month before I even got the call. Car accident, if you wanted to know. Guess his new woman didn't know about us until she started cleaning out their place."

"Sounds like Waylon." Dash shook his head and swallowed down more of his drink. "Fucker never could own up to anything."

His brother lifted his bottle in sardonic agreement.

Dash palmed the envelope. He frowned when there was more heft than a letter and thumbed open the tucked flap. A few bills were packaged inside.

"His estate," Seth grunted and took a swig from his bottle.

Dash shook his head. And that was that. The entirety of Waylon Asher's life boiled down to a couple hundred bucks and two pissed off men drinking together in a seedy bar.

Fuck. He didn't want to end up like his father.

"You ever get worried you can't outrun him? Like

he's always there, breathing down your neck, encouraging you to make the worst move possible?"

He slid a look at the man and grimaced. Fuck. He should have kept his damn mouth shut. He didn't know him from Adam. He could be a consortium sympathizer and wish death on humans. That crowd —Waylon included—would pop their fucking tops if they knew his gorgeous mate had a bear under her skin.

But hell. Seth was probably the only one he could talk to. Trent didn't approve because he didn't want a war between Crowleys and Ashfords. Lindley would scowl and ask a million questions and take Trent's side. Rhys's grunts and glares were good for a fight, but advice needed a few more syllables.

"Every damn day," Seth answered quietly. "He made me think the world had turned a corner when he stepped into my life. It had, he just made every-thing worse."

"I never thought I'd find a place to settle. Weeks, sometimes more, that was all I could stand of a place before I wanted to move on. That's how we lived. Seemed normal at the time. Seemed normal to continue when I cut ties." Dash ran his thumb along the edge of the label on his bottle. "It's different here.

Was. I thought I'd found somewhere to make my own, but now I'm not so sure."

"Ah, I see," his brother said with a small smile. "You have a woman."

"Colette, she's… she's…" He shrugged. "She's everything."

"Your mate?" Seth asked quietly.

"Yeah. Maybe." Dash made a face and shrugged a shoulder. "I feel it, but she won't admit it. Or maybe I'm just cursed and she doesn't feel it at all."

He hated the static in his brain. Why the hell did Trent and Lindley have it so easy with their mates? They'd gone out and hit their obstacles in the face, then got to claiming. He'd have gladly punched a thousand lions in the damn dick if it made Colette happy.

"Then what the hell are you doing here?"

Dash cocked his head. She needed space, but that didn't mean he needed to keep his distance. Physically, anyway. If she wouldn't talk, fine. But he could still be there for her. If he had to sit at the foot of her walls for the rest of his life, he would.

"Fuck if I know."

But he had an idea of where to go next.

CHAPTER 16

"Trouble, I heard. Such a shame, too." The elderly boar shifter clucked her tongue, then took a sip of her tea. "Pretty thing like that would've had her choice of suitors in our day."

Suitors were not her problem. She had one chasing after her long after she told him to get lost. And the other one? Well, she'd woken that morning to her brother banging a fist on her door and yelling at her to get rid of the damn lion once again sleeping on their porch.

In much harsher words.

Colette gritted her teeth to keep from snapping at the Old Maids seated in the prime window spot of Mug Shot. They'd been squatting in the coffee shop when she arrived and still squatted two hours later.

While she'd been mostly productive putting together her resume and starting her job search, they'd done nothing but clack their knitting needles and judge everyone who passed by the window.

The lull of passersby didn't stop their mouths. They'd simply switched targets to other patrons.

She needed to get the hell out of Bearden.

Colette ignored the objections of her inner bear as she scrolled through job listings. Her head throbbed with the constant fight for control. Dumb beast. She'd been thrilled to spot the lion lurking around the house the first morning. By the second, she'd been ready to roll over and let him do as he willed.

Colette glanced out a window and narrowed her eyes. She'd hoped getting off the ranch would lose her tail, but nope. Dash didn't even bother hiding around a corner. He sat in his truck, bouncing his eyes over everyone strolling along Main Street. As she glared, he spotted her and winked. Winked!

Claws slashed at her insides, roars vibrated her brain. Her heart ached, her muscles and joints complained and cracked with her every move, and her bear continued to go nuts.

The general discomfort and unease about leaving

had morphed into a strong desire to stay, with Dash at the helm.

Colette growled at her inner animal. Not happening.

Agitation crawled down her spine and set her teeth on edge. She wanted to bite something. Hard.

She hated that she couldn't let Dash in. More still, she hated that Jason wouldn't leave her the hell alone.

Easier to bottle up all her frustration and focus on getting out of town. She didn't need to stick in Bearden to feel miserable. She could take *that* with her wherever she went.

Her wry smile didn't last long before a roll of her eyes set in. Colette clamped down on her bear's urge to run and leap into the arms of the man who'd wormed his way into her every second thought. She needed to get out of Bearden and put her rules back into place.

Nothing serious. Nothing long term. Nothing at all, really. Staying alone sounded a little better every day. She had to protect herself from assholes like Jason and temptations like Dash.

Letting go of a harsh breath, she clicked open another potential listing and scanned down the page.

Ranch hand needed for the upcoming season, yada yada yada.

Three lines in, she nodded. At the fifth, she felt the tickle of a proper smile at the corners of her mouth.

Colette scrolled further, then growled.

Right there, under all the tasks and qualifications, were big, bold letters.

SUPERNATURALS NEED NOT APPLY.

There was no hiding her furry side when her name was on the registration list. A simple search would pull up all her details. Even if she somehow got in before her information worked through the database, people talked. She'd face more fines and another job search if she lied.

Which put her right back where she was. Alone, in a coffee shop, looking for a way to escape her brother's clan filled with happy mates and a bear determined to shove her toward a lion who saw a fight everywhere he turned.

Balls.

Her phone vibrated on the table next to her. She glanced over, doused the flicker of hope that Dash's name lit up the screen, then scowled when she spotted her lawyer's details instead.

Dark cloud hanging over her head, she stilled her

hand. What was the worst that could happen if she didn't answer immediately? She'd be forced to put her life on hold because her stalker decided to make another move and sent home to live in her old bedroom? She was already trapped exactly where she didn't want to be, and her usual distraction wanted to slip his fangs into her skin to mark her as his.

Yeah, one more missed call wasn't going to be the end of the world.

The bell above the door jerked her out of her head. Colette glanced up, on edge and expecting Jason, to see the third worst sight behind both men she wanted to avoid: the females of Dash's pride.

She knew Hailey from crashing her Christmas party, and it wasn't too difficult to identify Kyla as the other talkative one. The third woman trailing just behind the others must have been Sage.

Colette shot a furious look to the man still idling outside. At least he had the decency to look abashed. She had no intention of being ganged up on, spied upon, or forced into interacting with him under the guise of joining his people.

She quickly stuffed her laptop into her bag and gulped down the rest of her drink, then rushed out the door.

"What do you think you're doing?"

Colette pulled up short as she hit the sidewalk, then spun around. "I'm sorry?" she asked in confusion.

Sage scuffed the toe of her shoe against the cement, then raised her eyes. "With Dash. What do you think you're doing with Dash?"

Colette folded her arms over her chest. "I'm not doing anything with him."

"That's the problem. You get him all wound up and excited, then break him down to nothing. It's not fair to him. He's a good man who doesn't deserve to be yanked around."

Her bear shoved to the surface, ready to chomp down on the woman. The beast did not like the way she talked about Dash. Too familiar. Too... protective. She had no business getting involved with her—

Colette yanked back on her inner bear's runaway thoughts. One part stuck with her. No business.

She gave Sage a quick once-over. "I don't know what you think is going on—"

"If he's your mate, he's your mate. There's no consideration needed. Most people would be happy to find that fated connection." Sorrow burst into her scent. "Don't squander the chance you've been given."

"He's yours if you want him," she snapped back.

A growl bubbled in her chest. Claws slashed her to ribbons as her bear rampaged through her mind. Sendings flashed, a vision of bleak, grey desolation all covered in ash. Her future, according to the beast.

Sage flashed the ghost of a smile before lowering her eyes again. "Not mine. Yours, I think. Yours, if you'd let him be."

Then she slipped back into the coffee shop.

Colette wanted to throw her hands in the air and scream.

Not hers. Never hers. Men and mates were trouble she couldn't handle on top of everything else. Not when she felt trapped and cornered and caged.

The thin thread of a delicious scent yanked her attention across the street. Colette met Dash's worried look as he nearly hung out his window trying to get a look at her.

She didn't throw her hands in the air. Not one bit. Nor did she stomp away from Mug Shot and the prying eyes staring at her from both sides of the street.

The cold didn't touch her. She was too angry and upset. She wanted to run. Her bear paced through her head with increasing agitation, slashing and clawing at her center with a fierce need to bite something.

A hand caught the strap of her bag and yanked her into an alley.

Colette whipped around and swallowed back the fear that rose in the back of her throat. She'd had people around her last night. Tansey and Sloan and an entire field office of agents the night he'd cost her everything.

Moonlight and forests, with threads of filth woven into the underlying notes, hit her full in the face like a blast of air from a suddenly unlidded dumpster. "What are you doing here?" she demanded.

"I told you," Jason said, stepping closer, "I'm not going anywhere without you."

He took another step toward her. Colette shot a glance over her shoulder. Five steps, maybe, to the mouth of the alley. She could even pound on the back doors of stores if she needed, or shift right there and slam a heavy paw across his face. She was safe. Mostly.

The physical protections she could manage didn't stop the crawl of skeletal fingers up her spine.

"I told you, I'm not interested."

"A lion, Colette? A fucking lion?" Jason shook his

head, lip curling up in disgust. "You know what their kind did."

"Are you kidding me?" Colette huffed an incredulous laugh. "You don't have the right to judge anyone, much less someone who had nothing to do with those attacks."

He went on as if he hadn't heard her. Maybe he hadn't, she didn't know. He certainly hadn't listened to her any of the other times she told him to back off. "We'll get out of here. I know a place we can go until all this lion trouble blows over."

"You're the last person I'd pick. You're the entire reason I'm here. I lost my job because of you. I'm living with my brother because of you. You don't get to ruin my life then waltz in like you had no hand in that!"

His expression darkened and Colette took a step back. She'd seen him angry. Hurt from rejection, too. Those were nothing to the storm written over his face.

The look he fixed her with was one of a monster ready to rip through a herd of cattle.

"You pushed me into that," he snarled. "You weren't supposed to take that job. You were supposed to make a home with my pack."

She unglued her tongue from the roof of her mouth. "Never—"

Jason steamrolled over her objections, stalking forward. "I'll take them all from you. I'll keep every last distraction from your pretty little head. I want your love, Colette. I always get what I want."

Colette took a step back, then another. He was so close. Real fear lodged in her throat.

The dangerous wolf shoved something at her. She tore her eyes away from his face long enough to glance down to what he held in his hand.

Pictures. A whole stack of them. She yanked them out of his grasp and flipped through, horror coiling in her stomach.

Ethan. Tansey. Joss and Hunter. Lorne and Sloan. Liv, Alex, Nora, Jesse. Her brother's clan weren't the only ones pictured. The last one showed Dash, clear as day.

"You're stalking them, too?" she whispered.

"I'm making sure you're safe. Why won't you let me keep you safe?"

As if she was the unreasonable one.

"What's going on?" Dash appeared at the head of the alley. His brows shot down and vicious anger swirled in the air. "Colette, are you okay?"

She spun around, not seeing anything. Someone

grabbed her arm. Growls burst into her ears. She yanked away and stumbled to put extra space between herself and anyone. They wouldn't be targets if she kept her distance.

She needed to get the hell out of Bearden before Jason hurt someone. Because of her. Because he destroyed her world when she didn't give him what he wanted.

Her bear roared, but the noise faded into the pounding of her pulse.

"Colette?"

She rounded on the speaker. Dash. On the sidewalk. People all around and no sign of Jason, but he'd been there. He'd watched her with others. He probably watched her right then.

She raised her hands and backed away. "Just leave me alone, okay?"

CHAPTER 17

Dash lounged in the middle of the yard between the Ashford house and the barn. He hadn't even moved when one of the bears—Alex, maybe? He didn't really care—held down his horn for what seemed like five minutes straight. Asshole had finally driven around him.

A little shakeup in ranch traffic patterns was easy compared to his true goal. He was trying to out-stubborn the prettiest bear in the entire world.

His feet itched. His ankles and knees ached like he'd been trapped in one position for too long. Sharp rebukes traveled up to his brain and demanded to move. A trick, he knew. The moment he let himself walk, pins and needles would surge through his body. The painful feeling wouldn't even have the decency to attack the spots that complained the most; his heart would bear the brunt of the torment.

He wouldn't give up. Not on her. Not on *them.* Something was wrong and he wouldn't let her face it alone.

That was what it meant to be mate material, dammit. Every time he thought he knew where they stood, some seismic shift knocked him on his ass and left him staring up at the sky. He needed to brush himself off and brace for the next wave, not disappear at the first sign of trouble.

The front door creaked open. For a split second, hope flooded his veins. He scrambled to his feet, only to be disappointed when Ethan sauntered onto the porch. The bear moved from one end to the other, taking his time inspecting not a damn thing, all the while throwing dark glances in Dash's direction.

"You idiot," the Ashford alpha said flatly.

Dash raised his lip in a snarl. Fuck, he wished the male would square up to him. He'd love a good, dirty fight.

Ethan flicked him off. "How long are you going to keep this up?"

Dash rolled back onto the ground. Maybe if he didn't move, they could both pretend he was dead and avoid any of whatever bullshit heart-to-heart the bear wanted to have.

No such luck.

"I don't know what trouble she's had," Ethan continued after a moment, "but something has been brewing for a while. She won't talk about it, though, but that's never been her way. She likes to pretend she's tougher than she is.

"I thought it was you, but she's a good shot. If she really wanted you gone, she'd put a hole in you instead of running around with you whenever she comes home. Even now, with your carcass stinking up the place for the last three days and a constant string of complaints out of her mouth, she won't actually get rid of you."

Well, that was oddly comforting coming from a man he routinely tried to piss off.

"I suppose that says as much as you trying to become a rug or a speed bump outside my front door. I'd say good luck, but I'm honestly not sure which one of you I like seeing tortured the most." Ethan shrugged, then pushed off the railing and stomped his way back to the door.

"By the way," he paused at the edge of the doorway, "you're terrible at this sentry duty. She slipped down the trellis under her window a half hour ago."

Dash sprang to his feet. He didn't wait for the other man to disappear inside before he tore around the other side of the house.

Huge breaths dragged her scent into his nose. He glanced up to the second floor. The light in her window had been turned off, but the sash wasn't fully closed. Footsteps marked the snow underneath, then quickly turned to paw prints topped with wicked claws.

Pride and amusement puffed out his chest. Slippery, devious woman.

Dash bolted after her, pushing himself hard as fat flakes started to fall. The snow had finally arrived.

Her trail carried him away from the ranch house, the barn, the smaller homes belonging to the rest of the clan. He crested the tops of hills and dipped down the other side, never faltering in his pursuit of his mate.

The thin tinge of a delicious scent turned thicker. Fresher. Dash pulled up short and inhaled deeply.

The itch in his feet and the needles stabbing away at his heart disappeared.

She was close. The piney scent of bear mingled with the tangy spices that were all Colette. He licked his lips, anxious for another taste. Her scent alone burned away all the dark, gloomy thoughts that clouded his mind. She was a breath of air after his lungs nearly burst underwater.

He scanned the distance and… there she was.

Black fur covered the powerful bear. She hugged the fence on the Ashford side of the territory line and raced through the night toward the old homestead.

Dash put on a burst of speed until he caught up with her. She swung her head until silver eyes glittered at him, then snarled a warning.

Oh, fuck that.

He tore after her again. He'd been put off again and again. They needed to have words like proper adults.

Failing that, they'd fight in fur and he'd take her bear-ass down. Then, they could talk.

He caught her again and raced neck and neck. There wasn't any dodging him when he kept her tight against the fence without any room to jump. She could run ahead or fall behind, but he'd be right there with her.

She growled and snapped at him.

Dash jerked away. Bits of his mane snagged in her teeth, and he let off a growl of his own.

Colette veered away, putting on an extra dose of speed.

Frustration built inside him as she ran. He'd given her space. Let her have all the time in the world. He'd learned long ago there was no getting through to her when she got her back up and went stubbornly quiet. He'd been all in from the moment he first caught her scent, but now he needed more.

She was his, and it was about damn time she admitted it.

Colette swerved when he got near and bolted when he tried to clip her legs out from under her. The light dusting of snow churned under her paws and kicked into the air behind her.

He launched himself onto her back. One fluid move wrapped his front legs around her neck, then twisted him over her side. He slammed to the ground, but she went down with him.

The gorgeous bear fought and snarled in his tight hold. He ran his tongue down her fur to soothe her, but that only seemed to piss her off more. His lion half chuffed with pride. Fierce woman, savage bear, she didn't make an easy catch.

He'd fight until his dying breath for her.

His shape shimmered and cracked as he flashed back from lion to human. Fur brushed against his sensitive skin, sparking a wave of heat through his entire frame. "Shift," he commanded in a rough voice.

The beast still rode him hard, wanting to press close to the intoxicating woman, wanting to hear her accept him, wanting... her.

He kicked the creature to the back of his head and let gold eyes fall over Colette. "Shift," he said again.

A growled worked out of her in protest, but the air crackled with energy. Fur receded and her limbs shrank as her bear packed herself away, leaving a breathless, gorgeous, wild woman pressed into the ground under him.

Dash swallowed hard as he pressed his nose into the crook of her neck. Heat blasted off her skin where they touched; cold tempered him where snow met him instead.

"Talk to me, baby," he mouthed against her skin. One taste had his cock hard and ready to sink deep into her.

"I have nothing to say," she gritted out.

"Maybe not in words," he rumbled against the vein pounding under his lips, "but I can hear your heart racing."

She squirmed under him, but the noise that left her mouth was far from disapproving.

He trailed a hand down the side of her body. His fingers itched to explore more than the skin of her hip, but he kept himself in check. "I can smell how much you want me, Colette. I can taste it on your skin."

Dash rolled his hips against her, drawing a shuddering breath out of her lungs. Fuck, that was what he wanted to hear. "What was that?" he asked smugly.

Colette growled, then shoved at him hard. She scrambled to her feet the moment he let her loose. Cheeks flushed, she refused to look at him. "Leave me alone, Dash."

"Stop running, Colette," he growled. His hands tightened at his sides as he pushed to his feet. Years of being kept on the outside made his heart fight to beat. "Why won't you let me in? Why won't you let me help?"

He didn't know what he expected. Some smartass reply. A deflection. Thousands more feet added to her already impressive walls.

She deflated as he watched. Her shoulders slumped, and she suddenly had a great interest in the ground under her feet. "Because," she whispered after a moment. The word sounded like it'd been pulled out of her. "Because it's safer. He won't ever stop."

He wasn't prepared for the burst of sadness that soured her scent or the frown that pulled down her full lips. Trouble, Ethan said. Trouble he'd missed until it was right under his nose.

How had he failed his mate so miserably?

Dash took a step closer. "Colette," he said softly.

She held out a hand to stop him, then glanced over her shoulder. "Can we go inside? I don't want to do this out in the snow." She flicked a look at him and added, "Or naked."

"If you insist," Dash smirked automatically while his lion tore him to shreds. The beast slashed and roared at him to fix whatever had troubled their mate, to kill everything that ever made her frown.

She shook her head, but the brief puff of amusement in her scent was all he needed. The edge taken from them both, he trudged toward the homestead on her heels.

Her very shapely… heels.

Colette shot him a dirty look over her shoulder as she fished above the door for the key. Once the door swung open, she stepped into the darkness on the other side.

A ball of sweatpants hit him square in the chest

before he made it over the threshold. Dash grumbled as he tugged them on, then followed her inside.

"I've never been in here before."

"Too busy using the outside as a scratching post?" she asked blandly.

He shrugged in a non-answer.

The place had been stripped bare, but he didn't know what he expected. No one had lived there for years. The bears kept it standing, but didn't put much more work into it than necessary. Still, the inside had good bones even if they were a little dusty.

His eyes immediately found Colette. She leaned against the counter in the gutted kitchen. A baggy shirt fluttered against the tops of her thighs. So easy to spin her around, hitch her shirt up, and—

He cut off his thoughts. As much as he wanted to soothe her, he didn't want to fall back into their ways. He wanted her words first.

Then he wanted to claim every inch of her so thoroughly no one would bother her again.

He took up a spot about a foot away. Still within easy reach, he reasoned with his inner lion roaring to wrap her in his arms, but far enough away to give her space.

"Will you tell me what's going on? Were you running to find him?"

He didn't dare breathe. He willed his heart to stop entirely.

"No. Never." She shook her head. "I just needed to get out of the house. I was feeling cooped up and unsteady."

"And now?"

"And now I'm feeling prodded." Colette arched an eyebrow, but there wasn't any heat in her words. Resignation, mostly, and her shoulders sagged after a second as her brave face slipped. She winced and looked away, then started in a stutter, "Jason is his name, and he's been stalking me for the better part of two years now."

Dash let off a snarl. Fire ignited in his gut, fueled with all the hate and fury he could muster. His inner beast wanted to track the asshole down and make him disappear.

Colette shot him a look that locked him in place, then continued, "It started innocently. He bumped into me on campus, then asked if I wanted to get coffee later. Five minutes in, I knew there wasn't anything between us.

"After that came the notes. The candy and flowers. Shit I didn't want or need, even if I'd been interested in him. I'd much rather get some booze and go mudding." She canted her head and made a face. "And maybe get some chocolate after."

Dash snorted. Pure Colette. She didn't fit into any boxes. She wasn't a tomboy or a girly-girl. She did her own thing and didn't give a shit what others thought. He loved that cool, unabashed confidence of a woman who knew what she liked.

She sobered before he could encourage her to keep going. "He stopped after a few months. I assumed that meant he'd finally gotten the message and moved on, but no such luck. There was always something else. Didn't matter that I got a mailbox across town or moved to a secure building or spent extra time in Bearden, he'd find ways to get to me. It was almost like he wanted to check in just to make sure I knew he was still out there."

Sendings flashed through his head. Red and death. So much red and death. He wanted to go back in time and wrap a hand around the little fucker's throat in the bar or snap his neck in the alley. Asshole wasn't competition, but he sure as shit was a danger.

"I was relieved when I got a job because it took me somewhere new. He knew I had family in Bearden. He knew where I went to college. I thought maybe, just maybe, I could shake him for good. He's the reason why I'm back."

Dash tightened his hold on the edge of the counter. "What happened?"

"Little things, again. Busted gates, downed fences. I could smell him. It was like this stench of rotting garbage was deep in my nose and nothing could get it out. Meanwhile, all the humans went about like nothing was wrong. I was so fucking sick of it all."

Her heavy sigh turned to a growl as frustration dumped into her scent. She pushed away from the counter and paced through the kitchen. Dash wanted to reach for her, soothe her, but he held back. There was more, and he didn't want to stand in his own way when she opened up.

"So I went looking for him. Found him, too. I told him there was no future between us, never had been, and he needed to move on. The next night, he ripped through the herd, killing dozens and injuring more. I shifted to stop him and outed myself." She paused in her attempt to wear a path into the floor and turned to him. Wild hair, wild eyes, but she lifted her chin in a challenge against the whole damn world. "I'm facing charges for animal cruelty, property damage, scaring little humans half to death, plus whatever the penalty is these days for existing as a shifter. Probably destroyed any chance at a job outside the enclave and that little *weasel* still thinks he's going to sweep me off my feet. It's bullshit."

That was the fight he wanted to see. Tough woman. Strong woman.

Too bad it was all an act.

She'd given him a glimpse behind her walls. The cool exterior she presented to everyone hid so much more than he imagined. He could see the weight she'd carried. Still carried. All he wanted to do was shoulder some of that burden for her.

Dash held out his hand and prayed to all the gods in the sky that she'd take it.

Colette dropped her eyes. One second slid into another before she delicately hovered her palm over his.

Dash closed his fingers around her wrist and pulled her tight against his chest. He rested his chin on her head and rubbed a hand up and down her back. "You don't have to do this alone," he told her fiercely. "You have me."

"He'll hurt you, Dash. He's threatened my family." She pressed her forehead to his chest. "He's convinced we're mates."

"That's not true, is it?" He leaned forward and pressed a chaste kiss to her lips. His lion surged inside him at even that amount of contact. Fangs pressed against his gums and his cock hardened so fast he wondered how he didn't feel faint. "You know he isn't."

Colette leaned back and slowly dragged her gaze up his chest. Silver pooled in the blue of her eyes as she wet her lips. "I know he isn't," she said slowly. "I used to think I didn't ever want a mate, but now…"

But now…? Quiet stretched between them. He didn't dare press her for more. She already sounded so defeated under all the bluster. She'd been skittish and angry and he just wanted to soothe her.

Dash crushed her in another tight hug. "You're not in this alone," he assured her again.

CHAPTER 18

A lone. She didn't need to be alone.

The word struck a chord within her, burrowing deep into her brain. The sound and feel and even taste of it passed through her bear with a shudder of satisfaction and rightness.

No, she didn't need to be alone when she had Dash. Not when he proved himself over and over. Just being with her was a risk that rolled off his shoulders. He'd literally tracked her down and dragged the words out of her after days of sticking by her whether she liked it or not. He proved with his actions and his words that he wouldn't back down when shit got tough.

She swallowed hard, tongue suddenly stuck to the roof of her mouth. Her bear seized control, pushed her closer to the lion who offered her his heart. She wanted to fall and fall and fall with him waiting to catch her at the end. So easy. So tempting.

The clear, bright, honest eyes he turned on her urged her to trust in everything he offered.

She wanted to believe. She wanted to give him everything. Ethan had found love and a good mate, why couldn't she?

She stood on the edge of a doorway again, and this time, she stepped through.

Colette stood on her tiptoes and pressed a gentle kiss to his mouth. "I'm not in this alone," she repeated his words back to him. "I don't know how to do this, but I want to try. With you."

The admission hung in the air for long seconds.

Madness. Utter madness. She had every reason to avoid getting close to another person, but Dash, rough, rowdy Dash, made her reconsider.

Her bear roared through her head, did a little jig, jumped backward through flaming hoops. The words were sheer victory for her inner animal who'd pushed and shoved and tried everything to meet that instinctual desire for the powerful lion.

His mouth widened in a grin and his scent burst with happiness. Satisfaction. Need. Baked earth and dark spices pooled with deep longing as he leaned forward to brush another kiss against her lips. "We'll figure it out as we go."

He sipped at her slowly. Desire sparked in her middle under the chaste brushes, ignited with another kiss, grew to an inferno when a growl rattled in his throat. Colette wrapped her arms around his neck and pulled him closer before he could ease away.

She wanted him. She needed him. The thought of going back to her cold room was unbearable when he was hot as a furnace and intoxicating as the strongest moonshine.

His hands tightened on her hips as his tongue swept into her mouth. Sure strokes were punctuated with darkly delicious groans that paired with her own needy pants. He rolled his hips against her, pressing his cock between them, and Colette was lost.

Every inch of her felt stretched too thin. On fire. Nerves sparked pleasure under every bump and brush of their bodies. The solid wall of his hard chest teased her sensitive breasts, arrowing more desire straight to her aching core.

"Dash," she breathed. "Need you."

He cupped her, finger barely sliding into her wet heat. His eyes glowed when he rolled them upwards to meet her look. "Is that where you need me, baby?" he asked, voice thick and full of his inner animal.

Colette bit down on her lower lip and nodded.

Dash's mouth hitched up at one side in a delicious, devious smirk. "Oh no," he told her with a slow shake of his head. "You've given me enough silent treatments. Tell me what you want."

She thought her brain would melt out of her ears. Hot man, sexy man, drawing her out. He always felt like she played with fire, but now she wanted to burn.

"Yes," she gasped. "That's where I need you."

He pumped into her slowly, then raised his eyes to hers once again. "And?"

Colette wet her lips. "Lick me," she commanded. "Let me ride your fingers. Make me come."

He growled sharply as he dropped to his knees and buried his head between her legs.

Colette let her head fall back with the first savage swipe of his tongue through her folds. A shudder passed through her at the second. Her breath heaved in her lungs as she… as she…

Dash growled again and pressed kisses to the insides of her thighs. His chuckle sounded dangerously smug when she groaned in frustration.

He didn't leave her needy for long. He urged her

up on the edge of the counter. Wide shoulders spread her for him, and the growl that rattled in his throat bubbled hot desire through her veins.

Dash feathered kisses up each of her thighs, then slid a finger inside her, groan pushing out of his lips.

Colette swallowed hard as he rolled his eyes upward to meet her gaze. Soft gold swirled in the center, brightening. Glowing. He leaned forward and blew a soft breath over her heated flesh, then swirled his tongue around her clit.

Torture. He tortured her. Sexy man. Strong man. Still too many clothes on. His slow, fluttering licks and purposeful pumps of his fingers were pure torture.

She twisted and writhed under his touch, urging him on. But she knew the game he played. "More," she demanded. "I need more."

A purr vibrated in his throat, through her, boiled pure bliss in her veins. The world narrowed down to their panted breaths. Pleasure spiraled higher and higher, building the pressure in her center. Need gripped her as she rolled her hips to meet his hand.

"That's it, baby," Dash growled against her. "Let me feel those legs shake. I know you want to come. Let me taste you. Let me feel you."

Another shudder worked through her. She dug

her hands into the counter to keep her balance. Every muscle in her body screwed down tight, ready, ready for that final release.

"Come, Colette. Come for me." He caught her clit between his lips, sucking and flicking her at the same time.

She threw her head back in a wordless cry, body shattering as pleasure detonated in her core.

GORGEOUS. Beautiful. Fucking amazing. He didn't have words pretty enough to describe her or coarse enough for all the things he wanted to do to her. Without words, he was left with the most primal of communication—his body.

Dash hooked his fingers under the thin fabric of her baggy shirt. He kissed her hard, fast, delving between her lips in a prelude for her needy, delicious heat. Inch by inch, more of her skin met his. Heat blasted off her where their bodies met and flesh touched.

He pulled back when he had the shirt bunched under her breasts. He stretched the cotton tight over her frame, then sawed it back and forth over the stiff peaks of her nipples.

"Dash," she whimpered.

"And ignore these?" He dragged the shirt over the hard buds again, then dropped his teasing to cup both breasts. Bending, he sucked one nipple between his lips through the cloth.

Colette wrapped her hand around the tent in his sweats and stroked him. "I want you inside me."

Not a request. Pure command. And one he desperately wanted to obey.

With a growl, he whipped her shirt over her head and kicked out of his sweats. His cock throbbed, the ache tied to his pounding heartbeat. His lion roared through his head with the urge to satisfy their mate's need.

He swung her around to bend over the counter, then skimmed his hands over her luscious body. Up her spine. Around her front. He palmed her breasts, rolling her nipples between his fingers. Colette caught her lip between her teeth, then threw a hooded look over her shoulder.

"Not enough for you, baby?" he asked with a smirk. He trailed a single finger down her spine, then to her hip. He ventured around her front again and between her legs to press against that hot little button sure to make her dance against him. "What about now?"

"Dash," she said with a growl he thought she meant to be intimidating. The noise just grabbed him by the balls and dried his mouth. "More."

Dash fisted his cock. Heat gathered in the base of his spine and throbbed through his shaft. He wanted to drive into her, take her hard and fast, feel her shatter around him.

He wanted to draw everything out and hear her beg.

He wanted… everything.

He notched the head of his cock against her entrance. Fuck, she was hot. Tight. He watched in utter awe as he disappeared inside her, then slid his eyes closed at the rush of pleasure that wrapped around him.

"Fuck," Dash groaned between clenched teeth.

He withdrew and thrust forward again, forcing himself to slow, but it was so hard. So fucking hard when her gorgeous ass bounced against him and her eyes flashed pure silver and her scent wrapped around him until there was nothing left in the entire world but Colette.

She met him stroke for stroke, pushing into his thrusts, breathing hard. Her muscles fluttered against his aching cock, slowly driving him mad.

Moonlight filtered through the windows, casting

shadows over her slick skin. He faltered, stuttering almost to a complete stop as his fangs punched out of his gums. His lion surged inside him, wanting to close the distance between them, mark her as their own.

Fuck anyone who thought otherwise. He'd see them driven off or dead before he gave up a life with Colette.

"Dash," she growled. Colette braced herself against the counter, shoving against it, seeking out the pleasure he'd denied.

Dash threw his head back with a groan. Perfect bear. Perfect mate.

He slammed into her hard, instincts swirling with feral need to give her more, then more again. His grunts mixed and mingled with her softer moans, both tripping toward a final release.

"Almost," she panted. "So close."

"Do it, baby," he urged. "Let me feel you come. Need to feel you fucking come."

His hips bucked faster. Harder. Then she was there, fingers digging into the counter and body clenching him in her tight grasp. He dug a hand into her hair and arched her back, claiming her mouth in a harsh kiss, swallowing her cries as he tumbled after her.

Dash dragged out every shudder and throb, rolling his hips against her until they were wrung dry. He collapsed against her back, mouthing his way over her shoulders.

Fuck, he'd missed her. Missed being in her. Around her. Breathing in her scent. He didn't want the night to end. Couldn't bear the thought of leaving her alone and defenseless against that assweasel who thought he stood a chance of taming her.

Colette couldn't be tamed or corralled or leashed. All a man could do was grab on for dear life and enjoy the ride.

"Come back to my den," he said.

Not even a heartbeat passed before his gorgeous mate nodded. She glanced over her shoulder, silver eyes glinting in the moonlight. "I thought you'd never ask."

CHAPTER 19

Ding, ding, ding!

The crowd roared as the bell clanged the end of the match. Some jumped to their feet and sent their drinks flying. Others stomped in place. Defeated looks and heads hanging in hands came from those who placed the wrong bet.

"Balls," Colette groaned next to him. "I thought I had that one."

Dash grinned and tapped a finger to his cheek. "Pay up."

"I demand double or nothing," she negotiated, smelling amused.

"Darlin', you're so far in the hole, you'll be chained to my bed for a week if you keep going. Not that I'll complain."

Her pupils blew wide and her scent twisted and thickened around him. His grin widened even more as his lion stretched languidly through him.

Taking her to the shifter fights had been a stroke of genius. They'd tried food and drinks. They'd tried just drinks. Hell, he'd needed to chase her through the last snow of winter to get her to talk to him.

He should have known the fights would have been a hit. Colette was a country girl at heart and a tough badass to her core. She wanted six-packs instead of flowers. A little blood and violence won out over dinner reservations. Mémé always told him to find a woman with a spine of steel, and that was his Colette.

His.

Not officially with a mate mark, but the mental claim was enough to send a shiver down his spine and make his dick hard.

She was his and no delusional asswipe would take her from him.

The fighters in the ring below stumbled out and swept down the narrow path toward the tiny locker room to clean off the blood and sweat. Like clock-work, the next match lined up and prepared to enter.

Dash slung his arm over her shoulders and traced his fingers lightly over her skin. His inner beast purred. Happy cat, happy man, he didn't see how the night could be better.

Worrying, that. Only one way to go when on top.

The thought disappeared as Colette snuggled closer. Nah, they were due some good luck. He'd knock on wood all damn day and would keep going until his knuckles were bruised and raw if he kept the smile on her face.

The first fighter, a bear, entered the cage as the announcer shouted over the rising mix of stomping feet and last minute bets. He slunk forward, shooting daggers to the crowd. Dash frowned. Boring.

The wolf who entered second was a little better. He at least pumped his fists in the air. Pounding his chest was a little much, but the crowd was desperate for any excitement after the limp noodle on the other side of the ring.

He turned his head and glanced down at the woman under his arm. Skies above, she was breathtaking. "All right, take your pick. Who's going to win this one?"

Colette pursed her lips. "My money is on the wolf."

Dash snorted. "Your body, you mean."

She jabbed him in the side with an elbow, but he didn't let her go.

Three quick rings sounded the start of the match. The bear and wolf lunged for each other and started with a free-for-all of punches and kicks. Nothing glamorous or showy about them, but Colette put her faith in the wrong fighter again.

"Watch the wolf's footwork. See how he shuffles? Step, shuffle, step?" Dash turned his head to catch her nod. "It keeps him light on his feet, but he overuses it and only goes the one direction. He favors one side and leaves the other open."

The other man picked that moment to be an excellent demonstrator. The shuffling wolf threw out a hard right, but the bear deflected and went in with his own blow, working the wolf over easily.

Dash winced when the wolf went down and didn't move. "And that's why you don't rely on your good arm. If anything, you need to work your weaker one more."

"I'm surprised you know all this stuff. I mean, I like a good fight, but I couldn't talk shop about it." She brought her bottle to her lips and slashed him a teasing look. "I thought everyone on your side of the fence were just meatheads."

Dash leaned in close and let his breath whisper against her ear. "I still have some surprises to show you."

Colette's breath hitched in her chest and a light flush colored her cheeks. He debated teasing her more or taking her out to his truck to work off some of her debt.

He pulled back instead, throwing her an innocent smile. He took a sip of his drink and gestured around the warehouse with his bottle. "I grew up in places like this all over the country. Whenever my moms got tired and wanted somewhere to sit and think for longer than thirty seconds, or when she and my old man were at each other's throats, she bustled us off to Louisiana to stay with my grandmother. Staying too long in one place made me want to run."

Colette cocked her head, eyebrows shooting together. "You've been here for a few years, haven't you?"

Shit. He should have known she'd piece that together. Smart bear.

Dash rubbed a hand over the back of his head. He had to balance being honest with not pushing too hard or fast. While he'd been ready to claim her properly after their first few words, she still hadn't committed to the idea. "I had my reasons," he said simply.

Colette's lips curved up in a small smile she

tried to hide with a sip of her beer. Her scent thickened and sweetened, making her smell pleased. His lion licked his paws in smug satisfaction.

"What happened to them?" she asked after a moment.

"Mom is still around, living in Mémé's old place and complaining about the heat more every year, but she refuses to let me get her any new window units. Mémé passed a few years ago. Even on her deathbed, she scolded me for not settling and depriving her of great-grandcubs." Dash snorted. Cantankerous old woman.

"And your dad?"

"Dead. For a couple months, I guess. I only found out a few days ago." He grimaced. "Fucker wasn't exactly forthcoming about his previous families. Took some time to track us down."

"Shit." Colette's scent burst with regret. "I'm sorry."

"Don't feel bad. He was a bastard, through and through. Broke my mom's heart and saddled me with a half-brother."

"That I understand. Not the extra sibling part, but not feeling bad." Her lips pressed into a thin line.

Dash held his breath. He waited for her to let him

in or shut him out, not sure which she'd pick. He knew what hoped, though. What he wanted.

"My father was… I mean, I love him. He was my father. But he wasn't a very good one. Ethan did most of the raising. He was just kind of… there." She twisted to face him and frowned down at her lap. "Logically, I understand where it all went wrong. He lost his mate, he couldn't recover. It's a threat every bonded pair faces."

Well, hello, more clues. No wonder she was so hesitant to accept a mate. She'd witnessed firsthand the possible destruction of a snapped bond. That, combined with the asshole hot on her trail, was a recipe for reluctance.

Dash nodded, not wanting to break her flow.

"But logic doesn't read you bedtimes stories or teach you how to drive. He was who he was, and that person wasn't the father I wanted."

"Yeah," Dash sighed. He rubbed his thumb against his palm just to give himself some way to ground the twisting, turning, sense of unease in his gut. "That's exactly it. You can hope and wish your heart out, but sometimes the person you want and the person who is there aren't the same."

Ding, ding, ding!

Dash looked up sharply. A whole damn fight had

passed while they were caught in their little bubble. The thin layer holding back reality pricked open and all the sounds and smells flooded his senses. Too much. They scraped at him like a hair shirt.

He cleaned his throat and nodded to her empty bottle. "You want another beer?"

"I'm good." She hesitated for a single heartbeat, then lifted her gorgeous blue eyes to his face. "I wouldn't mind getting out of here."

Dash squeezed her thigh, then pushed to his feet. He dropped a hand down for her to take and pulled her upright. Somewhere quiet and alone sounded just fine to him, too.

They were halfway down the bleachers when he spotted Seth climbing toward them.

"Motherfucker," he cursed under his breath. Colette stiffened behind him and he twisted. "This fool coming our way is the brother I told you about."

Her eyebrows tried to reach her hairline, and she leaned around him to get a better look. "He was at the bar the other night."

"When you got crazy hot and possessive?" Dash teased. She scrunched her nose at him in answer.

"Dash," Seth greeted. "Didn't know you were watching the fights tonight."

"Aw, yeah. Needed something to do with

Colette." He pressed himself to the side to make room for her in the conversation. "Seth, Colette. Colette, Seth."

"Colette?" Seth's eyes widened and his mouth drew up in a relaxed smile. "Nice to meet you. I've heard—"

Dash growled a warning. Dumbfuck better not say a damn word to ruin his night.

Tangy, delighted amusement swirled in Colette's scent. "Good things, I hope," she said lightly. She flicked a glance to Dash, then back to Seth. "Buy me a drink sometime and I'll tell you all the bad about this one."

Seth barked a laugh. "Deal. I'll buy two, and we can get started right now."

Dash growled again and tugged her a little closer. "We were just leaving."

"Rain check, then." Seth canted his head to Colette, then fixed his gaze of Dash. "I'll see you next week when I nose in where I don't belong."

"We'll be saying our goodbyes in a week and a handful of hours, then. If you can tough it *that* long," Dash hit back with a casual shrug as he and Colette made their way around the other man.

"You're already acting like brothers," Colette said as they reached the parking lot.

"You think?"

"Oh yeah. Being a sibling is about ninety percent giving each other shit and seven percent undying, irrational support."

He quirked an eyebrow at her as he opened the truck door. "You're missing a few points."

"Oh, no," she said matter-of-factly, climbing into her seat. "That's for the murder you'll want to commit."

Dash snorted and shut her inside.

His lion paced inside him, but the beast didn't feel unsteady. A little high strung, some general nerves, but nothing like the itch that gripped him during his roughest moments.

The night had gone well. Suspiciously well. He had his mate at his side and she wasn't shooting him daggers. His pride consisted of fuckups and misfits that made him feel at home. Even his shiny, new brother hadn't felt like a burden.

He didn't want to poke and prod too much. Everything seemed caught for the moment and dangling by a thread. The slightest breeze threatened to snap the load entirely.

But he wanted more.

More of Colette. More of the weird back and forth with his kin. More of feeling like he belonged with the Crowley pride. They were the hopes and dreams of a man who could stay in one place longer than a few days and didn't have the poison of his father running through his veins.

Dash dreaded the itch in his feet returning.

Colette watched him from the corner of her eye the entire drive back to her house. The quiet between them didn't stab or antagonize. It was like a blanket fresh out of the dry wrapping around his shoulders. Gentle and warm. Comforting. Right.

This was what life was supposed to look like. Booze and fun and family and a good woman at his side.

He had to keep her. For his own sake, he had to figure out how to keep her and make all the other parts of his life work.

Dash held her tight as he walked her up to the door. Her scent wrapped around him and puffed up his inner lion.

"You make me want to stop running," he whispered against her lips.

Colette inhaled sharply as his first sip. A little burr rumbled in her chest, almost like the purr vibrating out of him. It took everything in him to keep from backing her against the wall and rolling those tight jeans down her legs, but he kept himself under control.

Barely.

He cupped her cheeks, running his thumbs over her skin, and tilted her head back. He sucked on her lower lip before licking into her mouth with complete abandon.

Dark pines and cinnamon coaxed and lured him into more, but he held steady. He wanted her total attention. He wanted her weak in the knees and hot for his touch.

His. She was his. And he'd hunt her even after she bore his mark on her skin.

Dash eased back with a small smack, then sipped at her slowly again. He couldn't help himself. She tasted too good.

He put a step between them when he resurfaced a second time.

Colette wobbled when he released her. She blinked once, twice, but even the third time didn't quite clear the glassy look from her eyes. Silver swirled in the center as she caught her balance against the door.

He took her hand and raised it to his lips. "Dream well," he told her, voice thick and low even to his own ears.

And he stepped off the porch.

"That's it?" she demanded. Her voice hardened with frustration. "You look like you're running right now."

Dash whipped around, hand going to imaginary pearls around his neck. He adopted his best scandalized tone. "What sort of man do you think I am? I don't give it up on the first date." He dropped the act with a sexy wink and stepped backward. "Besides, there's a difference between a tactical retreat and running. See you tomorrow, baby."

CHAPTER 20

Colette bounded down the stairs, feeling lighter and more refreshed than any morning since she arrived back on the ranch. The weight on her shoulders had been lifted, she'd made it through a real, actual date with Dash without ruining things, and her bear hadn't slashed her to ribbons or stolen her skin to run wild in the night.

The morning felt… good. Right. Hopeful and covered in glittery, sparkly goodness she'd be cleaning up for years to come.

As long as she didn't think about her lack of a job. Or her upcoming court date. Nope, better to keep focused on her in-town distraction that had tackled her into seeing him less as a distraction and more as something serious.

Colette crammed down the swelling panic, kicked over her rising walls like they were made of sand, and screeched to a halt when she entered the kitchen.

"What are you doing?" she asked the two women hard at some mischief she was certain she wanted no part of.

"Inventory," Tansey answered. She wobbled on a chair before catching herself against the cabinet. "Our first round of guests are due to arrive at the end of the month. Joss, you're entirely wrong. There isn't any rice up here."

"Are you sure? Look again," Joss said in a muffled voice, entire upper body stuck inside a cabinet. "I was sure we had an extra bag."

"I've looked five times. Unless you parceled it out in the overnight packs like a crazy person, we're out."

"The only thing in the overnight packs was the entirety of the cookout gear that *someone* said they already took out to scrub off the dust," Joss muttered.

Tansey smiled pleasantly at Colette. "As you can see, we have everything under control. Those need to be your exact words if your brother asks."

Colette lifted her hands and backed away slowly. "I wouldn't dare say otherwise."

"Smart girl," her brother's mate said, opening another cabinet.

She fled out the front door before either woman enlisted her in the madness of running a B&B, only to startle with the shrill ring of her phone.

Colette waved a greeting to her brother and his second poking their heads out of the barn, then dug her phone out of her pocket.

Balls.

Not the man she absolutely wasn't hoping to hear from.

Well, she was turning over a new leaf and confronting all the big scary things she'd avoided since being forced back home. Talking to her lawyer was just one more item to cross off her list.

She took a deep breath and connected the call. "This is Colette."

"Colette, Lacy Fairweather. Nice to finally hear from you. You've been ducking my calls," said a pleasant female voice with a hint of amusement.

"I, uhm," Colette deflected. Shit. She had been. Denying it would just be a lie. "I'm sorry. I've been meaning to get back in touch."

"Great!" came the answer. "I have time to meet

today. And I just happen to be in town, so how about we meet for coffee?"

Colette frowned. Every inch of her revolted being forced into action, but Dash was right. She couldn't keep herself locked behind a wall. The rest of the world still existed, and with it, her legal troubles. She needed to put on her big girl panties and deal with her messes.

"I can be there," she said. "Just give me a time and place."

COLETTE BOUNCED her eyes over the tables. The Old Maids held down the front table, as usual. A mom group chatted amongst themselves in another cluster. Townsfolk she'd known practically from birth filled up all but one of the tables.

She waved a greeting to Mug Shot's owner, Faith, then made a beeline for the unfamiliar face.

The woman had set up shop and turned her table into a mobile office. Her phone sat next to a large cup of coffee and a half-eaten cinnamon roll. A bag rested on the seat between her and the wall, the top flipped open and file folders visible inside. She scanned through documents from another folder and only looked up when Colette approached her.

That had to be the lawyer.

She flashed a bright smile and held up a manicured finger to ward off any introductions, then tapped an earpiece Colette missed on her first inspection. "That simply won't work for us. My client is an outstanding member of his community. He takes his mother to the grocery store every week, pays for his little sister's cello lessons, and volunteers regularly at a local animal shelter. This is not a man who would purposefully expose himself to campers. He went for an outing in his other form and shifted before discovering his clothes had been stolen. A common prank pulled on—and by—skinny dipping teens, I'm told."

She pulled a dongle away from her ear and moved her hair over her ear, but the voice on the other end was audible. "Ms. Fairweather, the park has postings forbidding use by shifters in any form—"

Ms. Fairweather inserted the piece back into her ear. "Which we will challenge as entirely discriminatory. He is a citizen by birth. He cannot be forbidden from public spaces."

Whatever was said in response brought another

smile to her face. "Perfect," she said, "I'll look for that paperwork this afternoon."

Colette waited while she ended the call, then slipped the dongle from her ear.

"My assistant," she said with a wry smile and a shake of the earpiece. "Work doesn't stop while I'm on the road. Plus, never hurts to drum up a little business wherever I go. Lacy Fairweather, at your service."

"Colette Ashford," she said, offering her hand.

Lacy took it in a surprisingly strong grip, then slid back into her seat. She gestured for Colette to settle on the opposite side of the table. "I'm so glad you didn't make me hunt you down myself. I always love a client who knows when to listen to good sense."

The leggy brunette was tall for a woman, with sharp features and an upturned nose. Her long hair hung around her shoulders, the flawless waves moving with her without a hint of a tangle. There was something about her, something that made Colette think of light and bubbles, almost like the embodiment of champagne.

Her eyebrows drew down in recognition. "You're fae."

"*Half*-fae, but the half is enough for the detractors." She shot a significant look toward the Old Maids furiously whispering in their usual spot. "Not that I can blame them, of course. Not with what happened here involving my people."

Her people—full-blooded fae—had attacked the town seeking to steal the Broken in some poorly conceived scheme to rip open the veil between worlds. They'd been convinced the sleeping figures held the key to returning to their rightful lands. How that could be, Colette wasn't sure. Insanity made anything seem possible, including a trip to a place not seen for so long that it may as well have been a fairytale.

Too bad their leader had kept just enough keen calculation about him to record an interview with a human reporter. When he didn't succeed, the reporter released the tape and revealed the existence of supernaturals to the entire world.

Lacy closed the file in front of her and slipped it into her bag, then slapped another on the table. "I've been reviewing your case as well as a few others for precedent. Bite marks, animal attacks, the like. We're in a legal revolution. Items more common in civil cases are starting to pop up in criminal court. You don't typically get 'my Muffy couldn't have bitten your precious four-year-old, and here's the bite record to prove it' when you're trying murderers."

Colette glanced around the coffee shop. No one seemed to pay them any mind, but she still shifted uncomfortably in her seat. Small towns were ripe with gossip. Bearden wasn't immune, and the biggest mouth-runners were seated on the other side of the room. "Should we be talking about this here?"

"Oh, don't worry." Lacy rested her elbow on the table and swirled her fingers closed into a loose fist.

A tingle washed over Colette's body. Pressure built in her ears, more and more, until she worked her jaw and it vanished with a pop.

"One of the bonuses of that half part. No one will know what we say. Unless you have a lip reader following you, in which case, you may have bigger problems," Lacy chuckled lightly as she flipped open the new file folder.

Colette tried to smile in return. She clamped down on her bear as the beast stirred. Another glance showed the rest of the coffee shop going about their conversations, but her main worry was the street outside. No lip reader. No Jason, either.

Still, would have been nice to have Dash posted up down the street just in case.

Lacy slid two photos across the table. "Can you tell me which of these were taken at the Walsh Ranch?"

Colette glanced down before wincing and looking away. "I don't know—"

"That's because you haven't looked," Lacy said sternly.

She slid the photos forward again and Colette forced herself to see the damage. Bite marks, meat. Fur tufted in the wrong direction. There was a difference between using an animal for food and a slaughter.

But something wasn't right. She pulled them both closer, trying to spot the difference.

"One is a bear, like yourself. Smaller than the bite records taken at the time of your detainment, which makes sense as it came from a photo of a carcass pulled off the internet. This one," she tapped one picture, "is an actual photo from the scene. What's interesting is they don't match at all. Oh, the gore is much the same, but when you get an expert in there, they can tell you one came from a bear and the other from—

"A wolf," Colette said on a breath.

Lacy folded her hands on the table and fixed

Colette with a knowing look. "A wolf, indeed. Was this another shifter?"

For the first time, Colette regarded her with respect. Just a few quick minutes, and she'd corralled her into an answer only one other person had heard.

Dash's words played through her head, soothing her bear and giving her courage.

You don't have to do this alone.

No, she didn't. She had Dash. She had her brother and his clan. Hell, she even had a lawyer willing to do her homework and meet her in her stomping grounds. She wasn't in this alone.

She'd tried her way, and Jason still found her. She'd tried respecting the old laws, and Jason murdered his alpha to get out from under an order to leave her alone. Her options to make him stop once and for all were limited.

"Yes," she said softly. Tension she hadn't realized she carried melted from her shoulders. "His name is Jason Waller, and he did it because he wanted to make me hurt."

Lacy listened carefully as she unloaded her story, occasionally stopping to take a note or ask for clarification.

"Okay," she said at the end. "So here's what we're going to do. I'm going to set up a meeting with the original Bozeman investigators and you're going to tell them everything you just told me. We'll bring our supporting documentation, like these pictures, any phone records you have, anything else you can think of, and give them the facts.

"The bite comparison should be enough to dismiss the destruction of property and animal cruelty charges. What's less clear is threatening the ranch owner. Mr. Walsh—"

Colette interrupted, "I was just trying to drive Jason off and save the herd. Myles shot me with a tranquilizer."

Lacy nodded. "If we still need to go before a judge, a lot depends on who we see. That may be seen as him having the upper hand, or being in such fear for his life he was forced to discharge a weapon to protect himself."

"And registering?"

"There's no getting around that, I'm afraid. The Bozeman SEA field office put you in the system the moment they carried you through the doors. You were living and working outside an enclave, and attended college before that. Unfair as it is, that's what we are forced to endure for the moment." Lacy grimaced. "If it were that alone, we could maybe fight the fines, but everything else considered, I would advise you to take the slap on the wrist if we can get the other charges dropped."

That was about what she expected. What she didn't expect was the calm inside her. There wasn't a deep rumble of panic over being trapped in Bearden. She jumped at pushing the blame on her inner animal, but that wasn't right, either.

More of Dash's words rolled through her head. He made her want to stop running.

"One more thing," Lacy said before Colette slunk out of her seat. "Do you have business casual in your closet? Slacks, jacket, neutral colors preferred, the whole shebang?"

Colette nodded.

"Perfect," Lacy continued. "What about a job?"

Colette sat back against her seat. "I've been applying, but nothing yet."

Lacy reached into her bag and pulled out a card. She scribbled a number down, then handed it to Colette. "Call my office and ask for Anna. She'll get you connected to someone who can help. Well-dressed and employed always plays better."

CHAPTER 21

D ash sat up, letting the blanket fall to his lap. He twisted around to pop open the lid on the cooler behind their heads. "Do you need another?"

Colette snaked an arm out from under the blanket and shook her bottle. Liquid sloshed inside. "Not yet."

She cozied back underneath and Dash couldn't help the slow grin that stretched his face. He'd dragged his mattress into the bed of his truck and packed a cooler with drinks. Steaks and potatoes stayed hot on the plates he'd wrapped with foil and stuck in a basket he'd bummed off Hailey. The moment Colette pulled up to his den, he'd hustled her into his truck and driven them to the far corner of the ranch for a picnic under the stars.

His lion was pleased, but he itched. Not in his feet or his legs. Somewhere deep in his gut and at the base of his skull twitched and trembled and skittered like the legs of an ant or the wings of a gnat. Barely there, almost invisible, those touches made him want to swat the back of his neck.

She'd laughed at his dumb jokes and didn't put a wall up between them, but something kept her distracted all night. He wanted to ignore the itch, but it was caught in the back of his mind. He felt trapped in place, waiting for the other shoe to drop.

She was there, but she didn't really *feel* there.

Had it been like that with his mother? Had Seth's mother felt the same? All the other women his father fooled into believing they were the only ones in his life?

He didn't think Colette had other families, no. But holding back as she'd done time and again were rooted in the same lack of truth and intimacy. He didn't want a repeat after she'd finally let him in.

Dash leaned back against the cooler and slowly sipped his beer. After a moment, Colette extricated herself from her blanket nest. Her shoulder and thigh brushed against his, firing off a wash of warmth through his body. Her soft, tangy scent filled his nose and made his mouth water.

Fucking hell, he wanted her. All of her. Body. Mind. Words. He'd let her dictate the rules and keep him at a distance for too long. He'd been given a taste of being with her completely. There was no going back for him.

"I met with the lawyer today," she said softly.

Dash turned, resting his arm on the cooler. "Is that where you've been all night?"

She ducked her face, then lifted her pretty blue eyes to meet his. "Sorry. It was just… a lot to deal with."

He reached forward and squeezed her hand. "I would have gone with you."

"I know. Thank you." She twisted her hand around to lace her fingers with his. "It was something I had to do alone."

He nodded, understanding and hating it at the same time. That fucker was still on the loose, and the quiet since he'd dragged Colette into the alley wasn't comforting in the slightest. It was another itch in the back of his mind.

His lion slunk through him, ready to prowl the night. Finding the little shitbird was a top priority.

Colette shifted around and matched his pose. "I told her everything," she said in a halting voice that picked up as she went. "About Jason stalking me, what happened the night I got picked up. That he's been here in town. She wants me to collect every scrap I still have, then we're going to meet with the agents again. She thinks there's a good chance of getting out from under everything."

"That's great!" Only, she didn't seem excited. She gave him the ghost of a smile that disappeared as quickly as it appeared. "There's more, isn't there?"

"She wants me to have a job to look respectable and told me to connect with someone at her office. So I did. I got put in touch with a ranch that's looking to fill a spot immediately. Nothing's official until we meet in person, but they sounded interested and didn't care about me being a shifter."

"But," Dash urged, hearing it in her voice and reading it in the stiffness of her body.

"But," she repeated with a tilt of her head. "It means moving. To South Dakota."

Her words hung in the air.

Dash swallowed the lump in his throat. There it was. The other damn shoe fell out of the sky and landed on his head.

She'd opened up and let him in. She'd stayed the night with him, in his den, in his bed. He still wasn't enough.

"Are you going to take it?" he asked in a neutral tone.

His lion, vicious, possessive beast, was everything but neutral. He roared and rampaged, sinking claws and fangs into Dash at every turn. He was a storm of hurt and regret and loss.

She was leaving. Again. Running right when things were starting to look good, backing away because she couldn't stand still.

Just like him.

Maybe it was for the best. He'd never dream of chaining her in place. She was too wild for that.

He could get back on the road, too. No cares, no worries, nothing but the next day ahead.

Nothing.

Nothing.

He was nothing without her.

THE AIR CHILLED AROUND COLETTE. No, she corrected. Not the air. Dash.

His scent just… vanished. Hard nothing replaced the baked earth and fresh soap, the same as hard nothing replaced any emotion in his eyes.

Balls. Her bear rolled through her with all the

usual demands to fix things with the man. Only there was no denying the beast. They'd been through too much, too fast. Colette had no resistance left.

Drained. She'd been drained when he sent his message asking for her to come to him. Between unloading her story for a second time, the reflex to look over her shoulder for Jason, and the sudden swing of good fortune in her favor, she'd hardly wanted to move from her bed. Besides, the troubling little detail of what to tell him made her want to hide until the problem went away.

But he was Dash. Her Dash. The man who'd chased her through the snow and tackled her to the ground just to figure out what was wrong. He'd stuck by her side when she tried to push him away; he deserved the same.

He wasn't Jason, who didn't listen to her and only wanted her as some trophy.

He wasn't her father, who made love and loss seem so intrinsically meshed that she rejected one for fear of the other.

Dash opened her heart in ways she didn't think were possible. He offered her a chance at the love she saw between Ethan and Tansey, and all the other mated pairs in her brother's clan. He was far from perfect… but so was she. They were imperfectly perfect for each other.

Her legal troubles loomed, and an escape hatch had appeared in the distance. She stood at a doorway, looking at an option where she made her own way outside of the enclave. No brother bothering her, no living in a house full of ghosts. She could shake off the dust of Bearden and restart her life.

Or she could do all that with Dash.

Colette locked eyes with him again. Gold churned in the grey with an unearthly glow.

She set her bottle down with great deliberation, then moved to straddle his lap. "I don't know," she answered, sliding her arms around his neck. "Can you think of a reason to stay?"

His hands landed on her hips, and he lifted his chin to meet her eyes. "I could think of a few," he drawled. He dragged the fingers of one hand up her arm. "Your family is here."

"I could always come visit them."

"We have delicious barbecue." He repeated the motion of her other arm. His hands dangled lightly over her shoulders as he leaned closer to kiss one corner of her mouth. "And where else are you going to find a town so serious about their made-up traditions?"

Colette huffed a laugh. "You're just scared the Ashfords are going to kick Crowley ass again with the Calving Celebration."

"We won last time, darlin'," he countered, kissed the other corner of her mouth. He nibbled a slow path over her lower lip. "The people aren't so bad here."

"No," she said softly. "Not so bad at all."

Dash threaded his fingers into her hair then and sipped at her. The careful deliberation claimed every bit of her mouth and sent heat bubbling in her veins. He was power, raw, beautiful, and all hers.

If she just took what he offered.

He curled his fingers under the hem of her shirt and dragged it up and over her head. Colette dropped her head back with a hiss as he dragged his tongue along the cups of her bra. Her nipples tightened to sharp buds before he even unsnapped and dragged the straps off her shoulders.

His large hands cupped her and he hummed with pure delight as he sucked one nipple, then the other, never leaving the other neglected with brushes of his fingers. Desire shot straight to her core until she couldn't keep herself from grinding her hips against him.

Dash landed his hands on her hips and pulled her

against him. "Little needy, baby?" he chuckled against her neck.

She didn't have the words to answer him. She leaned into him, pressing a kiss to his lips. He shot a hand up and tangled his fingers into her hair, holding her tight. His tongue swept over her lip until she gave him entrance, then he devoured her like a man starved. He licked and bit and stroked his tongue against her own, all the while rocking his hard length between her thighs in a perfect tease of what was to come.

Colette dragged her nails down his naked chest and the stacks of muscles lining his stomach. She worked open his jeans and pushed to her knees. With a wicked glint in her eyes, she freed his cock and wiggled down until she was between his legs.

She sucked him between her lips, flattening her tongue and taking him deep into her mouth. His salty taste exploded over her taste buds and dragged a reedy moan from her chest.

Dash's hands tightened in her hair. "Fuck, baby," he groaned, "make that noise again."

She bobbed on him, once, twice, then slowly eased back. She ran her tongue around his tip, teasing his head, lapping at the drops of pre-cum she created. His hips jerked and his jaw clenched, but he didn't push her for more.

Colette swallowed him down again. She wrapped her hand around his shaft and stroked what she couldn't fit between her lips. Achy desperation swirled through her center with each grunt and groan she dragged out of the sexy lion.

With a growl, Dash jerked his hips away. "Jeans off. Now," he snarled, pure desire thickening his words.

Fuck yes.

She shimmied out of her jeans and lifted up on her elbows, ready to climb him like a tree and slide down his impressive length, but then Dash was there, dropping between her legs. Pure gold churned in the eyes he roamed down her body. He wet his lips and growled when he reached the apex of her thighs.

Gripping himself, he rubbed his cock along her seam. "This where you want me?" he asked in a voice thick with his inner animal. He pulled back enough to tap her clit, then rubbed his head against her again. "Or do you need it, baby?"

"Need," she breathed. She needed him to fill her, stretch her, move so deep inside she couldn't tell where he ended and she began. She wanted to quake around him and feel the warmth when he growled her name.

His rumble—halfway between a purr and a growl—rocked through her the same moment he thrust forward, filling her in a solid stroke.

Colette arched against the delicious invasion and caught her lip between her teeth when he immediately retreated. His hands wrapped around her thighs and held her apart as he pounded into her hard and fast.

Pressure built in her core and fire raced through her veins. Dash dropped a hand and stroked her clit, pushing her even higher. She writhed under him as he drove her relentlessly toward her release.

"This," he growled. "This is all yours."

"Yes," Colette cried as she felt bliss rise up to claim her.

Their hips met against and again, the sound of flesh coming together filling the dark night around them.

And then he tumbled forward, denying her.

He slid an arm under her, around her, until his hand gripped her shoulder and held her close. So close. So fucking close, and he somehow loomed even larger.

Colette hardly dared to breathe.

She loved it. Loved the feel of his skin slick against her own. Loved his hot breath on her neck. The way his eyes caught hers and made her feel like she stared right into his very soul.

"Where you go, I go," he mouthed against her, punctuating the words with slow thrusts.

Colette nodded. A whine of frustration built inside her. He'd strung her out, then slowed his pace. This was... more. More than getting off, more than fun and distractions. He was imprinting himself on her and making sure she'd never forget him.

As if that was a problem.

His scent filled her nose, her lungs. The air made its way to her heart and pumped him through her veins. He was a part of her that she couldn't let go.

"Together," she breathed. "Whatever happens, we do together."

She moved with him, hips rising to meet his slow thrusts. Sighs pulled from her with his retreats. The gentle slide and roll of his hips swelled desperate pleasure inside her.

Colette dragged her nails up his neck and pulled him into a hard kiss. She wrapped her legs around him, pulling him closer.

"Close, Dash," she gasped.

"Yes," he said with a nip against her shoulder.

She shuddered, knowing exactly what he wanted. What he'd give her. When she told him she was ready.

Almost.

He bucked into her, the slow pace turning into a hard pounding. She clenched around him, feeling every drag and press and throb between them.

"Come," he ordered. He didn't stop this time, didn't hold her on the edge. "Come for me. Let me hear how much you love this."

Colette arched against him, a low moan slipping from her lips. Her entire body seemed to tremble under the pressure he'd conjured inside her. Pressure that was ready to spring. Pressure that dotted stars in her vision when she finally shattered.

"Yes," Dash growled, cocky laugh mixing with his own groan.

He grabbed her hips and thrust into her harder than before, fucking through her orgasm until he froze inside her and warmth throbbed.

Dash collapsed on top of her, then rolled to the side and dragged her against him. He draped his leg over her and tucked her even closer before nuzzling his chin against her shoulder.

And there was just something… right about that.

CHAPTER 22

When Colette pulled to a stop in front of Dash's den, a huge white lion and a tawny beast with a black mane were slapping each other wherever they could reach. Lunging, yanking back at the last second, feinting and slipping past blind spots, they bled one another until the last patches of snow in their yards turned to mud like the rest of the land in the precursor to actual spring.

Her truck rocked and slid with the force of one of the beasts clipping the side.

Oh, hell no. She still had payments to make!

She dropped out the door and slammed it shut behind her, rounding the hood in a second. "Shift back, assholes! Don't you *dare* go near my truck again!"

"Good luck," Kyla called from her porch.

Colette jumped. She hadn't noticed the woman there at first, but chalked it up to utter insanity. She had a foot propped against the railing, a bottle of nail polish in her hand, and wobbled as she tried to keep her balance and apply color to her toenails.

"They've been going at it for twenty minutes!" she added, squeaked, and tumbled to the ground. "I'm okay! Oh, this is a better position..."

Colette bit back her giggle and made a mental note to go through Tansey's supplies for ideas for a pedicure care package.

She fixed another glare on the two lions who still hadn't shifted. Summoning all the power of her bear, she jabbed a finger at them. "Now!"

Shapes shimmered and cracked apart until Dash and Rhys pushed to their feet. Rhys had the good grace of disappearing into his den, but Dash approached her with his hands stretched out appeasingly.

"Hey, darlin'," Dash said lightly. "When did you get here?"

"As if you didn't see the big truck you slammed into?" she growled again.

"It was more of a graze?"

Colette snorted, and a grin broke out over Dash's

face. He dropped his hands and went to his truck, pulling out a pair of jeans. Her inner bear rumbled with appreciation watching him tug them on, then stalked toward her.

He cupped her cheeks and pressed a small kiss to her lips. "You made it in time for dinner."

Colette glanced at the mess she'd avoided when she drove up and promptly forgot in the defense of her truck. Mismatched tables were placed in a single line in the center of the dens. Chairs that didn't look like they paired with any of the tables ringed the dining hall monstrosity guaranteed to make any formal dinner guest run screaming in the other direction.

"What's all this?"

"Oh, this?" He waved vaguely at the tables. "Just a little something I put together."

"I thought I heard someone pull up!" Hailey called before Colette could say anything. "Are they finally done fighting?"

"Colette ordered them back to two feet. I vote she's our alpha now," Kyla called.

"Seconded," Dash added.

"Thirded," Trent rumbled as he joined Hailey on the porch with a huge plate in his hands. "Congrats, they're your mess now. The keys to the asylum will be at the front desk."

Dash wrapped an arm around her waist and hauled her close to his side. "I think that means you're on the approved visitor's list."

"No," Trent snorted. "That means she's in charge. I never said any of you fuckers could bring someone home." He set the plate in the center of the table, then pointed at Hailey, Kyla, then Sage. "And yet, here you all are."

The first drew a huffed laugh from Hailey and glares from Lindley and Rhys as they made their way out of their dens.

Dash grinned and held Colette a little tighter. "I mean, if you wanna fuckin' fight about it…"

Hailey edged in as a growl left Trent. "Now, now, kitty cats," she scolded, smelling wickedly amused, "no brawling at the dinner table."

Crazy. Mad. Absolutely insane. Colette loved the sharp, untamed edge they had to them.

Hailey clapped her hands and set everyone to work bringing out more plates of food and making sure enough drinks were close at hand.

The bickering almost, almost, stopped when everyone had full plates. Almost.

If you didn't count Dash popping the bottom of

Rhys's beer. Or Lindley flicking rice at Sage. Colette half expected to see Trent with his head in his hands by the time they were done.

She leaned back and rubbed a hand over the food baby she'd nurtured into existence with piles of enchiladas and fajitas. Pitchers of margaritas helped wash down every delicious bite.

Dash nudged her elbow. "You training to start a career as a sumo wrestler?"

Trent glanced around. "Mud wrestling, maybe." He smirked at Hailey. "I wouldn't mind watching that."

Hailey slapped his arm. "Trent Crowley, I would take you down in an instant."

"Like you beat me in a snowball fight? Wait…" He tapped a finger to his chin, then gave her a sly look. "I won that."

"Only because you had help. And then cheated. Dirty double-crosser," Hailey sniped back without any heat in her words.

Trent answered by slinging an arm over her shoulders and drawing her close for a kiss.

Colette ducked her face to hide her growing smile. Sendings flashed, Dash and herself overlapping the cuteness of Trent and Hailey, or Lindley and Kyla. Even the slow, sneaking looks between Rhys and Sage that she wasn't sure anyone else noticed. Every last one of them were starting points for her bear's desires.

Hers, too.

She turned to find Dash looking at her with gold churning in his eyes, one corner of his mouth hitched up. Butterflies took flight in her stomach as she reached for his hand and squeezed. "So that's a no on the wrestling," she said to everyone else, "but how about mudding?"

The guys all looked at each other, then back to her.

"Are you serious?" Lindley asked.

"What would Ethan say?" Trent added with a frown.

Colette shrugged. "It's half mine. What's he going to do, disown me?"

Lindley pointed at her, then Dash. Deadly serious, he told him, "Don't fuck this up."

Complete innocence washed over Dash's face before he narrowed his eyes at the pride's second. Colette let off a laugh and pushed to her feet before the two could dive over the table and start another brawl.

Messy lions. Crazy lions. She loved every second of their wild antics.

The caravan of trucks bumped down the ranch road, then streaked past the entrance of Black Claw Ranch. Colette jumped out of Dash's truck as soon as he pulled to a stop in front of the closed gate on the far edge of the Ashford property.

Her brother, and their father before them, and the owners before that, all kept the strip of land leading into the mountains fenced off from the rest of the grazing pastures. Spring snowmelt and summer storms turned the ground soft and muddy and perfect for getting dirty.

Colette slipped back into her seat and pointed straight ahead. "Let's go!"

Dash eased through the fence with the others right behind him. While he carefully crept forward, they gunned past with loud honks.

He hit the first curve long after the others were lost over the hills. Colette eyed him, then the track ahead, then Dash again.

"What are you doing?"

"Obeying the rules of the road," he muttered. "Keeping you safe."

"Now is not the time to get protective of me!"

He wheeled around slowly, barely throwing any mud into the air. The engine worked hard to crest him over the low hill, then they bounced into a puddle on the other side.

Lights flashed behind them as another truck roared toward them on their second pass. Colette watched as Trent gunned forward, jumping the same hill and landing next to them with a big splash. He twisted the steering wheel around and threw a big arc of mud against the side of Dash's truck, then screamed off down the track.

And Dash still crawled along another bump and corrected a skid that would have at least shaken them around a bit.

"Stop the truck. Stop the truck!"

Dash slammed on the breaks and she jerked against the seatbelt for the first time. "What's wrong?"

"What's wrong?" she asked flatly. "Really? You're driving like an old granny here. Are we mudding or are we driving around looking at gardens?"

He frowned, but she clicked her seatbelt open. "Scoot over," she told him, kicking open her door. "If you want something done right, you have to do it yourself."

"You are not driving my truck," he protested when she opened his door.

"I most certainly am. Someone has to because

you're clearly not." She stroked a hand over the armrest inside the door. "Poor baby just wants to spin her wheels."

He glowered at her before climbing into the passenger's seat. She ignored the grumblings as she loaded herself behind the wheel and moved the seat forward to accommodate her shorter legs. She glanced to make sure he'd buckled up, then slammed her foot on the gas with a whooped laugh.

Dash grabbed the oh-shit bar above the window as she whipped down the track. They slipped and skidded up and down hills, bumped into ruts hidden under the puddles, and revved forward until they caught the taillights of Trent's truck.

She didn't stop even then. A yank of the steering wheel spun them around and repaid the mud bath they'd taken earlier. Trent shook his fist at them through his window while Hailey threw her head back with a laugh.

Colette lost count of how many times they raced through the track. It was hard to tally when Dash kept her in fits of laughter by narrating her driving or insulting the others, let alone the winces and white-knuckled grips to steady himself when he thought she took a turn too fast.

All the trucks were covered with mud from front

to back by the time they arrived back on the Crowley ranch.

"Who wants dessert?" Hailey called when Trent helped her down to the ground.

Colette's hand went into the air along with everyone else's.

"I don't think I've ever been more attracted to you than this moment," Dash chuckled at her side.

She slashed an indulgent look in his direction. "Keep it in your pants, buddy."

He cupped her cheeks and brushed his lips against hers once, twice, then sank into a slow, deep kiss that curled her toes.

"Okay," he taunted when he eased back. "If that's what you really want."

Colette's growl sputtered to nothing when he grabbed her hand and pulled her around to follow the rest of the pride back toward the tables in the middle of the yard.

Her bear stirred inside her. She expected something cranky from the beast, being surrounded by two mated pairs. A third, if her betting wasn't as off with people as it'd been with fighting matches.

Her entire filled with warmth until she felt like she'd burst. It stuck to her ribs and packed the empty spaces she thought would never patch over, much less feel complete.

The night, the man at her side… every last part of it felt right.

"I like them," she said quietly.

Dash turned his head. "I do, too."

No joking. Not even the little hint of a tease. Just pure, honest truth in his words and scent.

Colette glanced at him, then back to the others. They were wild, but so was he. Foulmouthed, crazy, hardworking when they got down to it, hard fighting when they didn't. Strong women tempered the savage men, and both sides made the others better.

They were his people, without a doubt. She didn't want to rip him away from the place he'd learned to call home.

Still quiet, she asked, "What if I—we stay?"

Dash turned to her fully. He crossed his arms over his chest and his expression shuttered. Guarded. So guarded. But a light, faint thread of hope infused his scent.

"You have your offer in South Dakota. I thought you wanted to go," he said in a measured tone.

"There will be other jobs. And yes, I wanted to escape when I left for college. There are too many bad memories and ghosts in my house. Ethan's changed a lot, but it still doesn't feel like home." She scuffed her shoe against the ground to encourage the words to unstick from her tongue. "I like how alive you make things feel."

Dash pulled her close and pressed his forehead to hers. A low purr rattled in his throat as he dragged her hand to rest over his heart. The steady thump matched her own.

"Can you feel that?" he asked in almost a whisper. "Can you feel my lion steadying out? That's all because of you."

Her bear stretched through her, feeling supremely pleased.

Colette reached for his hand and covered her own heart. "You, too."

CHAPTER 23

Colette let go of a sigh of relief the moment she stepped out into the late afternoon sunlight. She tilted her face to the sky and grinned widely as her bear slunk through her with sendings and impressions of victory.

It wasn't over, but she'd finally taken steps in the right direction. No more brambles tearing at her skin; she'd found her way to a clear path forward.

Soon, she wouldn't need to worry about Jason. Her legal troubles were all but resolved. There was nothing else for her to do but drive home to Bearden.

Home. Bearden. Two words that hadn't fit together just a couple short weeks ago. Now she couldn't imagine anything different.

Oh, there wasn't any magic bullet that fixed all her problems. No magic wand or pixie dust washed over all the old hurts. She knew she'd still stumble and skin her knees and trip back into the brambles, but she didn't need to pick herself up by herself. Not anymore.

"Congratulations," Lacy said beside her. "That went well."

Understatement of the century.

All charges dropped. Those three magic words would forever be branded across her mind. She hadn't attacked Myles Walsh, she hadn't killed his cattle, and any property damage was because of Jason.

Myles had wanted to fight the human endangerment charge, but Lacy pointed out the uphill battle he'd face. He hadn't been injured, he'd successfully knocked Colette unconscious, and she'd simply been trying to keep him and his herd safe.

She still had to pay fines for existing as a shifter outside the registration list, but the fine was a small price to pay once the other charges disappeared.

"I overheard the agents making a call to the local SEA office serving the area where the Waller pack resides," her lawyer said. "How are you doing with all this?"

Colette winced. "My pockets feel much lighter, but I'm good. This feels right."

"I'll be happy to take a little more off you when we get this completely settled," Lacy said lightly. "Until then, keep your nose clean. Call if you have any trouble, otherwise I'll be in touch once the additional proceedings can be scheduled."

Colette resisted the urge to pirouette across the parking lot. She wasn't a freaking ballerina; she'd probably just fall on her ass. Instead, she calmly, *calmly,* walked toward her truck.

And wiggled in her front seat until an unmarked car pulled into a spot next to her and two agents stared.

Containing her excitement, Colette tugged her blouse straight, started her engine, and began her drive home.

Home, and to Dash.

Her bear stirred at the mere mention of the sexy lion. He was so, so bad for her. And so, so good. She didn't need the strong, stoic type who never showed any emotion. She wanted the man who made her laugh, made her come, and made her happy. He'd made her realize she didn't need to protect herself and keep her walls up. No one could predict the future, but he'd proven he'd stick by her side no matter what.

Colette hummed happily, anxious to drive past the offensive Crowley Ranch signs telling her to GO AWAY and FUCK OFF, then frowned.

Someone followed her.

She wasn't sure at first. Then she rationalized they were simply headed north, the same as her.

Colette adjusted her mirror and split her focus between the cars ahead and the ones behind. Every mile, it seemed, a black SUV three vehicles back nosed into the shoulder, then straightened in their lane.

Maybe they didn't want her. Maybe they were trying to keep an eye on someone else while they followed them to a nice, innocent family gathering.

Her gut didn't believe a word of the lies her brain provided.

The empty gas tank signal decided that moment was the opportune time to mock her with a bright light.

Yeah, fuck everything about that. She was pretty damn certain she had more than half a tank left when she arrived in Bozeman.

She reached for her phone nestled in the cup holder,

but hands slick with sweat and shaky with nerves fumbled the device. Feeling a lifeline slip away, Colette watched her phone skid under the passenger's seat.

"Fuck me," she grumbled. She tried to reach it, keep an eye on the cars ahead, the SUV behind her, and nearly swerved off the side of the road.

Her stomach churned and the empty tank light glowered at her.

Balls. No choice, she whipped through traffic, trying to add some extra space between herself and her tail. Glancing in her mirror, ahead, over her shoulder, she didn't stop until she hit the next exit and rolled into the first gas station.

She circled the pumps and edged into the empty one closest to the exit. Getting back on the road was a top priority, even if she turned out to be completely paranoid.

And if she didn't? Well, any delay seemed like a mistake.

Colette jumped out of her truck, armed with her credit card and keys sandwiched between her fingers for a quick weapon. She fiddled with the keypad and slammed the nozzle into her tank to glug down as much gas as she dared.

A black SUV pulled into the gas station.

"Shit." Colette grimaced and ducked behind the pump.

The vehicle rolled to a stop on the opposite side of the machine. The driver jumped out and made a beeline for the store.

Colette rubbed the heel of her hand over her heart. Paranoid. Absolutely paranoid. Talking about Jason had her jumpy as hell. No one was going to stop for snacks before they got on with the stalking.

She let go of a heavy sigh. Her hands shook as she settled the pump back into place.

The man who'd entered the convenience store came back out, empty-handed.

"Ma'am?" someone asked from the front of her truck.

Colette jerked her attention around just as the rear door of the SUV popped open. Something pinched the back of her neck. She tried to raise her hand, but it felt like she waded through cement.

"What—?" she started thickly.

The world spun, and she slumped against the side of her truck.

An arm wrapped around her. The thick stench of garbage made her want to hurl.

Darkness descended, and she was no more.

COLETTE JERKED AWAKE. She tried smacking at whatever tickled her nose, but she couldn't move her hands.

She couldn't move her feet, either.

The sharp, pungent odor under her nose didn't disappear until she snapped her eyes open on a face she never wanted to see again.

Jason.

She struggled against her bonds again, letting her gaze drop. She was seated in a chair, wrists and ankles bound to the arms and legs. They should have snapped. Should have fallen away to the floor and let her rip through the bastard with the stupid smirk on his face.

She reached for her bear, but only the faint sense of fur brushed against her mind.

He'd fucking chained her with silver.

Asshole.

Colette snapped her eyes back to Jason's face and snarled

"There's my sugar," Jason chuckled. He cupped her cheek with a clammy hand. "That's the fight I need in my mate."

"I'm not your mate. I will never be your mate."

She strained at her bonds again, shaking her head in denial and to clear his rotten garbage scent from her nose. "When will you get that through your head?"

Jason stepped away. "That's just the lion talking. I told you to stay away from him. He's no good for you, Colette. He's poisoned your mind against me."

Her words died on her tongue. Behind Jason, beyond his hot garbage scent, he'd set a table. Candles, flowers, wine glasses and iced waters. Plates were covered with mirrored domes to hide the bounty underneath. Crispy bread waited to be sliced and buttered. The presentation would have been nice if the situation hadn't been fifty shades of fucked up.

She glanced around at the rest of the shack. The tiny kitchenette claimed part of a wall. He hadn't even bothered to make the twin bed in one corner, instead leaving the rumbled blankets thrown to one side in psychopath romantic chic. One door and one window looked like her only options for escape if she could ever get free of the shackles around her wrists.

She reached for her bear again. Useless. Absolutely useless. Her other half was trapped deep inside her head.

Jason returned a second later and laid a needle in

line with the silverware at his place setting. "What's in that?" Colette asked, fighting to keep her voice steady.

He rounded the table, eyes glinting in the candle-light. He smoothed a hand over her hair, then dragged his touch down her arm, lingering when he reached her hand. "Just a little something to keep you calm, should you need it again."

Colette curled her fingers under as much as possible. Her skin crawled at the touch. Her stomach turned with his scent. Asshole had kidnapped her. She didn't want to hold his fucking hand.

"Don't be upset with me, sugar. We'll be home with our pack soon enough." He flashed her a watery smile. "They've been waiting for you for so long."

"I don't want to go anywhere with you," she gritted out.

"You can't stay away from your mate." He turned from her again and lifted the domes from the plates. Steaks and sides were underneath. "We'll eat, then you can meet our guard. I handpicked the toughest enforcers to guarantee you're never left unprotected again."

More like never given the chance to get away.

"Our cubs, too, will stay safe. We'll go back to our pack lands. We'll stay there until all this lion business blows over. No need to worry about any consortium fucks banding together to make war. No humans to mistreat you. We'll be happy there, I swear. You, me, our cubs, our pack. We'll be happy."

"I am not your mate," she told him again. The walls pressed down on her, tightening her chest. She wanted to close her eyes and disappear. "My mate is in Bearden."

Colette hated that Jason was the first to hear the words. He'd snatched her safety and security. He'd taken her trust. And now he stole words that should have belonged to Dash.

Dash was everything she needed, and everything she saw slipping out of her fingers.

Jason's face darkened. He shoved to his feet and stalked to the door. Yanking it open, he growled into the air, "Bring me the tablet."

The door shoved wide as another wolf stepped inside.

"Stop him," Colette pleaded. She didn't know what else to do. She was tied down and had no animal to call on. Hell, no one even knew she was missing. Wouldn't until she didn't show up in a few hours. "I don't know what crazy he's told you, but I'm not his mate. I don't want to be here. I just want to go home."

A muscle jumped along his jaw, but he didn't say a word. He pulled a tablet out of a bag hanging from his shoulder, poked around on the screen, then handed it to Jason.

"It's amazing what you can pick up at the store these days," Jason said as if he hadn't heard her.

Maybe he hadn't. Maybe whatever sickness had hold of his brain couldn't process outright rejection.

His steps back to her seat were like nails being driven into her coffin. He leaned against the table and carefully propped the tablet against her untouched glasses of water and wine.

"What is that?" she demanded. Her stomach turned with sickening realization as her brain slowly caught up to what her eyes saw. She wanted to go back to those moments of delay when she could still deny what Jason had on the screen.

Dash.

He stood on the edge of the barn, arms crossed over his chest as he chatted with the others of his pride. The video wasn't the highest quality, but she could clearly see the relaxed way the men stood. They simply went about their business, not a hint they were being watched.

Still daylight, she noted. So she hadn't been taken very far.

Colette twisted away from the tablet. "I don't know what sick games you're playing—"

Jason grabbed her face and forced her to look at the screen. "This is on you. Remember that. You forced my hand."

"What does that mean?" she demanded. "What are you doing?"

Jason snapped his fingers and pointed at his wolf. "Get Chester on the phone. Wait for my signal."

Colette blanched under the frigid tone. Her stomach sank like a stone, the rope around her feet dragging her down with it. Her bear, weak and faint, clawed to escape the prison of silver that held her captive. "No. Don't do this. Don't you fucking do this!"

Jason pulled her phone from his pocket and dialed a number, putting it on speaker for her to hear. "Watch carefully," he ordered with a jerk of his chin toward the tablet.

The last of her doubt and hope that the video was anything but a live feed slipped away. Dash flicked the others off and walked away several steps, fishing into his pocket. She could just about see the smile on his face as he recognized her number.

"Hey, darlin'," he greeted. "How'd it go?"

Dread filled her. Her heart stuttered, faltered, collapsed in on itself like a dead star.

"Dash!" she yelled. "Get out of there!"

Jason backhanded her hard enough to make her cheek throb. "You should have left her alone, lion. She never belonged to you."

Dash stiffened on the screen. "Where the fuck is Colette?"

He never got his answer. Jason lifted his eyes to the other wolf with a phone pressed to his ear, then disconnected Colette's phone. "Take the shot."

The feed adjusted, lined Dash up in the exact center…

And went dead.

CHAPTER 24

Dash snarled into the dead line. He tightened his hand around the phone and wanted to chuck it far from him.

Motherfucker.

That asshole had Colette. He'd heard her in the background, the muffled words sounding like she was on speaker. His lion rampaged through him, ready to tear the world apart until he had her safe in his grasp. Then the real destruction would begin. He'd bathe in the blood of anyone who tried to keep them apart—

The whizz of a bullet streamed by his ear and thunked into a fence post, throwing the pride into turmoil and chaos with him at the center.

"What the fuck?" Lindley yelled.

"Get down!" Trent ordered with a wave of his hands.

Dash didn't listen. He snarled and bolted in the direction the shot had originated.

His lion ripped through him between one step and the next. Two feet turned to four paws that ate up the ground and killed the distance between him and the fucker who'd stolen his mate. He could already taste the blood on his tongue when he ripped the throats out of everyone involved.

Colette belonged to him.

The burr of an engine put more speed into his legs. He soared over the dips and hills of the ranch, chasing that sound.

A truck careened around the corner. Seth drove like a madman, snarl plastered on his face. He caught sight of Dash, then shoved a finger forward, not slowing in the slightest.

Dash turned and followed only when he caught sight of a man bouncing in the bed of the truck.

Seth didn't stop, didn't even slow, until he reached the barn. He slammed the brakes hard enough to skid his entire truck sideways, then jumped out, leaving his door hanging open.

"Saw this one nosing around on my way up here, so I thought I'd score some early points and see what he was doing." Seth hauled the man out of the bed of his truck. "I knew you had enemies when I took the job. I didn't know getting shot at was part of the deal."

Dash didn't hear him. Blind rage had a hand around his throat. He raced into the yard, growling, snarling, ready to reach out a paw and snag flesh.

Trent stepped into his path and forced him to pull up short.

"Shift," his alpha ordered. His eyes flashed gold with his inner beast. "Shift and get dressed. You can't go killing him until you know what he has to say."

Power infused the words, but his beast bucked against the alpha order. The animal part of him wanted to slash through Trent to get to the fucker on the other side. He'd kill them all to bring the asshole to justice.

"Shift," Trent growled, throwing more weight into the word.

With a roar of pain and fury, Dash's shape ripped apart and left him shaking and panting in the dirt. He threw a murderous look to Trent, then pushed himself upright on wobbling legs. He marched stiffly to his truck and shoved himself into the change of clothes he kept inside.

The extra seconds didn't do a damn thing to calm

him. He stalked forward and threw a punch hard enough to stagger the man in Seth's grasp.

"Where the fuck is she?" he demanded. Another punch doubled the man over. The scent of fur and moonlight burst into the air. The identifiers marking him as a wolf vaguely brushed through his head; his lion roared them away.

Lion. Bear. Salmon that'd flop on the ground. What he had under his skin didn't matter. He just needed a working set of vocal cords.

He kicked the wolf's knee and dropped him to the ground. "Where the fuck did he take her?"

The wolf tried to crawl away. Dash reared back and kicked him hard in the side, flipping the bastard over. He brought his foot down on his ribs, his stomach. He wanted to hear every damn bone in his body break.

Trent jumped in front of him. Strong arms wrapped around his middle and dragged him away. Seth, some distant part of his brain told him. His brother was there to hold him back.

"Easy," Trent growled, a firm hand pressing against his chest. "Easy."

Easy? *Easy?* No such fucking word when his mate was gone. He didn't know if she was alive or dead. "They have my mate," he ground out.

His lion rippled through him. Claws bit into the hands he balled at his sides. Fur brushed under his skin. The beast wanted out. Wanted to tear into the man and feast on his fear.

"We'll get her back," Trent assured him in a fierce voice. "We'll find her. You're not in this alone."

Breath coming hard, Dash dipped his chin once. He threw up his hands in surrender and shuffled back as soon as Trent and Seth let him loose.

Not alone. He wasn't alone. He had his pride. Hell, he even had his brother. They were all on his side. They'd help him rip Colette out of wherever she'd been taken. He just had to be smart, think things through. Then he could go murder kitty on their asses.

"Where was he, exactly?" Trent asked Seth.

"I saw him cross the fence not far from the ranch entrance. He had a van parked about a quarter-mile away, unless someone else happened to break down in the same area. I didn't stop to take a close look. I chased his scent and found him lining up a shot." Seth nudged him with his foot. "He had a camera of some sort with him, too."

"Go," Trent ordered Rhys. A massive white lion burst out of the man as he streaked in the direction Seth pointed.

"Cowards," Dash muttered. He glared at the wolf sprawled in the dirt. "The boss is too afraid to do his own dirty work. The pissant peons are too afraid to get their hands messy."

Something about the man tickled his memory. He wasn't from Bearden, that was for damn sure. No one in their right mind would dare rile up the rough and rowdy lions on the edge of the territory. No one would take their fucking mates.

"I've seen him before."

The others stilled. No pacing, no restless shifting from foot to foot. Every face turned to him.

"I've seen him before," he said again. Dash squatted in front of the wolf. "Fight night with Colette. He was in the ring. Got his ass handed to him by a bear."

Colette bet on him. Too bad for his master he was as useless with a gun as he'd been in the ring.

"I think I've seen him, too. More than once." Seth cocked his head, then slowly nodded. "If he's working the circuit, maybe he's shacking up in one of their cabins."

The wolf stiffened. Dash zeroed in on the gesture. His lion knew weakness when he smelled the blood in the water.

He shrugged a shoulder, staring straight into the

bastard's face with cold, dead eyes. "You might as well tell us where you've stashed my mate. Dicking us around isn't going to go well for you."

"You think you're the only one? He's been watching all of you." He wheezed a laugh, then grimaced in pain, holding his side. "He'll take everyone from her until he's the only one she has left."

Trent snarled, then shoved a finger at Lindley. "Get word to the women. Tell them to drop everything and get somewhere safe." He yanked his phone from his pocket and dialed a number. "Get your ass over here, bear. Your sister has been taken and I'm not sure how long I can keep Dash on the leash."

Not long. Not long at all. Dash bared his teeth and snarled at the wolf. "And we'll take one of you for every hurt she suffers."

CHAPTER 25

"What happened?" Jason demanded. He whirled on the other wolf and shook the blank tablet at him. "What the fuck happened!"

The wolf took the device and poked at the options. "I don't know," he said in a panicky tone. "The feed should be working."

He shrank back under Jason's frown, but Colette laughed.

"You idiots," she said, laughing again. Deep, deep inside her, fur brushed against her fingers. Caution, strength, she didn't know which. She'd never been one to keep her mouth shut, either. Facing down the end of her life wasn't the time to learn. The stubborn streak that added steel to her spine wouldn't allow her to bend for some dickhole who thought he could abduct her into loving him. "You've been found out. Your man is probably spilling his guts to the Crowley pride this minute. And after they've wrung him dry, he'll *see* his guts spilled on the dirt at his feet."

Jason stared at her, his lips pressing together tighter and tighter until he looked like he had a little puckered asshole on his face. Cold fury whipped off him, dropping the temperature by ten degrees and lifting goose bumps up and down her arms.

"Prepare the others," he ordered. "I want a tight perimeter. It's obvious we can't stay here. The ties of this place are too strong for her to bear."

"They're coming for you," she told the other wolf. "You should run while you still can."

Jason growled and jabbed a finger to the door. "Out!"

The wolf's shoulders slumped under the weight of alpha power. Colette frowned at the unnecessary display. Uncontrolled, maybe. Either way, her brother never resorted to using his place in the clan so casually.

Jason stalked forward, eyes glowing with madness. "You were so strong the first time I saw you. Beautiful. Strutting around like you owned the world. I loved the power you carried with you. I wanted to own it."

Not love or cherish. Own.

Colette's stomach turned at the idea. She wasn't a person to him. Her thoughts and feelings didn't matter, though that had been clear the first time he disregarded her rejection. She was something to be possessed.

How different he was from Dash. Dash would have followed her to a different state to see her happy with a job she wanted. He hadn't discouraged her from leaving Bearden for school. He'd bit his tongue to hide the heartache he felt when they were apart. Dash held her up; there was no *owning* her.

If she made it out alive, she'd sink her fangs in his skin so fast, his head would spin.

If. Big, huge, if with her wrists and ankles secured to a chair and her bear trapped deep in her mind.

Jason rounded the table and leaned against it. "I've been patient with you," he murmured and stroked a hand down her hair. His other hand reached for the other side of the table. "I see now that you need a strong hand. You will not contradict me in front of the pack again, do you understand?"

"Don't touch me!" she snapped. Colette jerked

out of his touch. Her eyes went wide when she saw what he'd been reaching for with his free hand.

Jason snarled and jammed the needle into her neck.

Once again, darkness washed over her.

DASH EYED the road that disappeared in the distance. Even with the windows rolled down, he couldn't sense a damn thing. Bugs sounded off in their evening orchestras. The wind rustled branches. But the scent of wolves? Any howls or human voices?

Nothing.

"You're sure this is the place?"

Seth nodded at his side. "First place I landed when I got here. It puts distance between the enclave and gives the fighters some privacy. If they're using the fighting ring as a cover, this is where they'd be."

"Wouldn't want any local law creeping up on you," Dash said flatly.

Seth shrugged and Dash let it go. Poking at the man wouldn't get him closer to Colette. Hell, he'd stayed in rundown hovels and shacks hidden away by the organizers, too. He was just pissed and frustrated that some fucklehead had stolen his mate out from under his nose.

He should have gone with her to that meeting her lawyer set up. He was big enough of a man to wait patiently in the car while she got her shit done. He'd even have brought a little cooler filled with itty bitty bottles of champagne and some of those tiny sandwiches to make a picnic celebration when she was done.

His lion swiped at him and cleared away the images in his head. He hadn't done that. And now he was left with a dirt road and no fucking idea if Colette was at the end of it.

No good came from sitting on his hands. Dash cracked open the door and dropped to the ground.

His lion ripped out of him, shape cracking and reforming with pops and snaps of pain. Dash shook off the moment of darkness as his mind readjusted from two-legged thinking to four and fangs.

His mate was close. He had to believe she was near. Alive. Breathing and cursing and ready to kick some wolf ass.

One deep inhale was all he allowed himself before bolting through the trees.

The wolves found him.

He scented them before he saw them. The moonlight and fur heavy in the air pushed him to run faster. The scents grew thicker as he entered their territory. Too many trails to count, too many to pick apart. The concentration pointed a big sign to where he needed to go.

And his wild run hopefully hid the arrival of the others.

He slowed as he neared a clearing, unease rolling down his spine.

Colette's truck was parked in front of a shack. Dash's heart squeezed down to nothing in his chest.

What if he'd been wrong?

No. There had to be an explanation. She'd yelled at him through the phone. That little shit of a stalker took her against her will. That her truck sat there was proof she was near.

He stepped into the clearing with a roar.

Howls rose up through the forest. More than he expected, but he didn't care. The roars of lions and bears answered their cries and sounded the beginning of the war.

Wolves rushed at him, streaking out of the shadows. They moved fast, swerved, bit, jumped in and out of range. He swiped and snapped and charged, but they pulled off and swarmed the lion to his left.

It was smart fighting, even if it left their backsides open to the attacks that barreled after them. The surge overwhelmed one, then shifted to a random target, again and again, never standing still long enough for a prolonged attack. Wolves were picked off, flung away. Some stopped moving where they fell, while others bolted back into the snapping rush.

Distractions. Necessary distractions. The lions and bears fought for him and Colette. They drew the teeth and claws away from him to find her, get her free, and maybe even taste a little blood on her behalf.

He lunged into the mix, dodging one wolf and slamming another away from him. The surge pushed his way and stopped only when Rhys's white beast roared loud enough to send a few wolves cowering to their bellies.

They didn't stay down for long. A lone howl rose up through the ranks. The sound caught another, then another, until nearly all the wolves lifted their snouts high in the air and added their voices in a song of death.

Dash knew exactly who raised the cry and who led the charge straight for him.

Fur flashed in every direction and suddenly the distractions split off and found new targets. Groups snapped at the heels of his people, lunged for their throats, jumped on their backs. As soon as one was ripped loose, another replaced it.

Dash turned and bolted for the shack, crashing his entire weight into the door. Wood ripped away from the frame and slammed into the creaky floor under his paws.

One sniff was all he needed to feel his hopes similarly crash and rip apart.

Shit. *Shit!*

No one was there. No bit of blonde hid around a corner or under the bed. Not a single whiff of her delicious scent.

She wasn't there.

Dash let off a vicious roar that promised death to whoever kept him from his mate and charged out of the small shack in time to see a lone wolf slip around the corner and flee the battle. The heavy stench of madness and garbage left an unmistakable trail.

Jason.

Dash made it three steps before a wave of fur and fangs crested over him. Teeth snapped at his paws, his shoulders, everywhere they could reach. They twisted under his feet to trip him down, then threw themselves at his soft underbelly.

No. It couldn't end this way. He couldn't lose

Colette with the sound of snarls ringing in his ears. They'd been given a chance, had that chance stolen from them. He couldn't stand to let the bastard that destroyed her faith in others be the one standing when the final bell rang.

Dash channeled all his strength into a final scramble for his feet. He didn't waste a second. As soon as he was free, he lunged after Jason.

He had to find Colette before that bastard won.

COLETTE JERKED awake to another round of powerful scents under her nose. She shook her head, trying to clear the grogginess that tried to drag her back down. She must not have been out for long or maybe the dose had been different. Every part of her felt worse than when she'd first awakened in her own private hell.

Fingers snapped in front of her face. She blinked hard and focused on the man crouched at her side. She'd seen him before. He'd been the one with the tablet.

A low growl worked out of her middle. She reached for her bear before remembering her inner beast had been denied to her.

"Listen to me," the wolf said frantically. "He's not your mate? You mean it?"

The words penetrated her fuzzy head.

And so did the sounds outside.

War. War and death had arrived, just as she predicted. Roars sounded all around the little shack. Sharper cries, too. Pain laced those sounds before turning to snarls or ceasing entirely.

"You think I'd go through all this just for fun?" Colette swept her gaze over the dim little room. Skies above, the sounds outside... Even one life lost was too much death and destruction for her to handle and all because Jason wouldn't leave her alone. "Smell me. Listen to me. I'm telling you the truth. I'll phrase it however you want, but you have to believe me."

He pressed the heel of his hand to his temple. "But he said... he told us..."

Colette swallowed hard. She had to make him believe. Whatever disgruntled alpha bullshit Jason had pulled on his pack, she had to break through. "He lied to you. I told him to stay away. He killed your previous alpha to get out from under the order to leave me alone. And now he's ordering all of you to follow him into death. Let me go. Let me get back to my mate. That's the only way you will survive."

She held her breath and hoped she cut through Jason's bullshit.

Something flickered over the man's face, then he reached for the straps holding her feet. "He's going to kill us all, just like you said."

She rolled one ankle, then the other the moment they were freed. Her heart jumped into her throat when he reached for one of her hands.

So close. So damn close. She could taste her freedom.

One strap fell away, and the door banged open.

Colette jumped in her seat as the other wolf scrambled to his feet. Eyes locked on Jason, she frantically worked open the final strap holding her in place.

"You, too?" Jason growled. "My own second would steal my mate from me?"

"She's not yours." He shook his head. "She's never been yours. You've been lying to us this entire time."

A muscle jumped along Jason's jaw and his eyes narrowed. "Lies. They've filled her head with lies."

"Not lies," Colette said.

She reached for her bear, but the feel of fur was still too distant. Silver in the straps, she'd thought, but he'd freed her from the chair and she still couldn't feel more than the vaguest sense of the beast. Whatever they'd dosed her with kept her inner animal locked down.

Colette cast another look around the room. Maybe she could find the needles Jason used to inject her. He could do with a little forced naptime. They'd all be better off if he wasn't spewing his garbage words into the world.

Or maybe she could just skip out the door and never look back.

Unlikely, with the two males facing off against one another, and her caught on the far side of the room.

"This needs to end," his second said in the testy silence.

"You're right about that," Jason snarled.

He moved fast, grabbing a knife from the table and slicing a line up his second's chest all in the same movement. The man stumbled forward and right into Jason's murderous arms. Another slice killed the light in his eyes.

Colette fought not to retch or sink into shock. He'd tried to help her. Fought against his alpha. And ended up shoved out the door like trash.

"You'll stay with me. I'll make sure of it," Jason said.

Holy hell. Colette ripped her eyes away from the

red on his hands. Jason stared at her without emotion. She wanted something to prove he was still human, still capable of remorse or regret, but his eyes were as dead as his second's.

Instinct screamed to get away from him.

He stepped closer. She backed away. The jerky dance kept the table between them.

Panic burrowed through her head. Into her heart. Her stomach twisted and knotted with each step backward. She hated feeling weak and right then, Jason made her feel small and pitiful.

She wanted her bear. She wanted Dash. Colette wanted to wake up from the nightmare she'd been stuffed inside.

She stepped back again, then again. Jason prowled around with her. She hoped, prayed, and wished with every fiber of her being she could see her plan to the end.

As soon as she rounded the table, she spun and rushed for the door. Her fingers closed around the cold metal of the knob and—

Jason grabbed her from behind and pinned her arms to her side. A hand fisted in her hair and yanked her head to expose her neck.

Colette shuddered at the hot breath bathing her skin. She struggled in his grip, desperate to get free.

She couldn't elbow him. He didn't do more than grunt when she stomped on his foot.

"You're mine," Jason said against her neck.

No. Not his. Never his. She'd rather die than accept Jason as her mate.

Fuck. She screwed her eyes closed and waited for the flash of pain and the death of her soul.

The door banged open and Colette's eyes flew open to see Dash striding inside.

His eyes flashed pure gold when he caught sight of her in Jason's arms. His face twisted into something terrible and full of hate. A savage snarl shook the air and stopped her heart in her chest.

"Dash," she whispered.

Her relief was short-lived as Jason flung her aside and lunged for her mate.

Both their forms broke apart in an instant, but Jason was a trifle slower. He paid with a snap of Dash's jaws around his tail.

Shit. Shit. There wasn't enough room for a lion and a wolf to rip into each other.

Colette scrambled back as the table toppled, then cracked into nothing. Silverware and those ridiculous domes skittered across the floor. Glasses shattered and crunched under heavy bodies and paws.

Jason jumped for Dash's throat, but the lion

jerked away and slammed out a paw. Jason yelped at the blow, then jumped right back into the attack.

They spun around again in a flurry of snapped jaws. Colette jumped onto the bed and crowded as far from the beasts as possible, trying to gauge the right moment to shoot for the door. She'd be flattened if she tried to stay inside.

Each time Jason jumped in, Dash sliced him a little more. Claws, fangs, didn't matter which. Jason was soon covered in his own blood, not at all a match for the huge lion that had wedged himself between the crazed wolf and her foot of safety in the corner.

Still, he didn't slow.

Then others were there, pushing and crowding the door. Ethan. Trent. Other lions and bears made themselves known. Jason couldn't hurt her with all her people so close.

It was a fact he couldn't accept.

With a whining snarl, he slipped around Dash and took one final lunge for her throat. Colette flinched away, arms going up to protect herself, but the teeth never reached her.

Dash snatched hold of the wolf by his neck and whipped him down to the floor. The loud crack of a broken neck ended his threats forever.

Hands cupped her cheeks and forced her to look into gold eyes. Concern flooded her nose, tinged underneath with moonlight and baked earth.

"Are you okay?" Dash asked in a voice thick with emotion. He stepped back, though he didn't drop his hands, and passed a look down her body.

Colette didn't say a word. She wrapped her arms around his waist and tucked her face against his chest.

Relief flooded through her at the purr that rattled in his throat. All the fear of never seeing him again, never touching him, faded in that moment. He was there. He was real. And she didn't need to fear losing him.

After a moment, Colette freed herself from Dash's arms and made herself look at Jason's still body for three long seconds. Then she straightened her shoulders and walked through the crowd of lions and bears that parted for her.

Fuck him and all his insane ideas. She'd never belonged to him.

Her place was with Dash.

CHAPTER 26

D ash idled at the edge of the dirt road leading up to the Crowley ranch. He glanced at Colette. She studiously stared out the window and he could only see a ghostly reflection of her shuttered eyes.

A growl kicked in his chest, the sound ratcheting up and down with each breath. He drummed his fingers against the steering wheel, still keyed up from the fight.

From almost losing her.

He shoved the thought aside with a harsh swipe of his hand through his head. He didn't want the reminder. He could have done without the reality, but being forced through it once was more than enough.

And now…? He didn't know where the fuck they stood.

Colette pressed her hand against his thigh. "Are *you* okay?"

He slashed his eyes to her. "Are you kidding? I nearly had a heart attack knowing that fucker got to you. I'd give my left nut to bring him back to life to kill him all over again. The right one, too." He scrubbed a hand down his face. "Fuck, just parcel me out and let's keep the blood flowing."

She cracked a smile, but the stiffness didn't leave her shoulders. And why would it? She'd been taken against her will and nearly had a mate forced on her. The fate was worse than death for a woman like Colette. She placed a good deal of pride in her ability to get shit done, and that fuckweasel cut her legs out from under her.

He'd give both nuts *and* an ear to snap that fucker's neck again.

"Where am I taking you?" he croaked.

Colette turned to him. Blue eyes found his, then sparked with a hint of silver. "Home," she said quietly. "Our home."

He cranked his head to look at her. Truth in her words. Her eyes. Her scent was clean of any doubt.

Without a word, mostly because his dumbfuck

brain didn't know what to say, he made the turn into Crowley territory.

Her hand never left his thigh.

His lion purred the entire stretch up the road, growing louder and louder. Electricity seemed to build in the air between them. Colette shifted in her seat, spearing him with tiny glances that made his inner beast preen.

His mate wanted to come home.

But silence hung heavy when he kicked the door shut behind them.

And why the fuck not? She'd been through too much.

He leaned against the door, arms folded over his chest, and watched as she paced from one end of the room to the other.

"Today—tonight," she grimaced at the clock on the microwave. They were barely into the dark hours. "It fucking sucked, okay? That's all there is to it. All the words in the world can't boil it down better than that."

Dash held out his hand and waited for her to take it. Heat flared to life the moment their skin connected. He drew her close and wrapped his arms around her.

There was nothing else he could do. The

bastard was dead, barring any self-sacrifice and reanimation. He could tend the bumps and bruises on her body, but the ones in her head were unreachable.

So he held her until her shoulders relaxed and her body shook. While her heart beat furiously in her chest. He held her until she turned her face up to meet his.

"He nearly claimed me," her mouth twisted on the words, "but you're the one I want."

"Colette," he breathed.

He cupped her cheeks, smoothing his thumbs over her skin. She pressed her hand to his heart. Static shocked him and kicked the organ back to life. Her scent billowed around him and inflated lungs that had gone flat the moment he heard her shout on the phone.

"Don't make me wait," she said with a nip of his lip. "I don't want anyone else thinking they can come between us."

His lion roared through his head, happy to honor her request without preamble. Just a wham, bam, thank-you-ma'am of a bite to bind them for life.

Dash slammed on the brakes. He wanted his mark on her skin, too, but he had to be smoother than that. He'd never forgive himself if he didn't make her shatter around him at least once before he slid his fangs into her flesh.

Colette stepped away from him. Fierce determination bloomed in her delicious scent. Her fingers brushed down the front of her silky shirt, working open the buttons. She toed off her shoes, then let her pants pool around her feet.

She stepped toward his room, throwing him a look over her shoulder. "Are you coming?"

Fuck yes.

He dropped his eyes to her perfect ass as she walked away from him. He yanked his shirt over his head and trailed after her. He kicked off one boot, then another. He lost his jeans somewhere in the hallway.

And found Colette naked in his bed, propped on her elbows, one ankle kicked over the other.

Gorgeous woman. Perfect image. Everything he wanted.

Except the shitty ordeal that put her there.

As if reading his thoughts, she arched an eyebrow. "I swear to all that's holy, Dash, if you make me wait, you'll be waiting for another year. I'm trusting you with my heart. Trust the decision I've made."

Dash kept his eyes locked on hers as he dropped

a knee to the bed, then slowly crawled up her body. He planted kisses along her thighs, her hips, between her breasts, drowning in the sweet arousal that wafted off her skin. Her pulse kicked up right along with her breathing.

"Oh, baby," he pulled back, one corner of his mouth hitching up in a lopsided grin, "you'll have to do better than that. I'm no stranger to waiting for you. I've had practice. A little more won't kill me."

Colette growled, eyes flashing with her frustration. She wrapped her arms around his neck and yanked him into a kiss that killed his laugh.

Kissing her was no joke.

Dash groaned at the first taste of her tongue against his. Their mouths clashed in a twisting tangle, seeking and giving, both trying to stave off the potential for loss they'd suffered through in just a few short hours. They were alive, together. They'd survived what had been thrown at them.

And now they were the ones to claim the rewards.

Dash kissed a path across her jaw and down her neck. He nipped at her skin, enjoying how she tightened her hands on his shoulders. There. Right there. He'd add his mark to her skin and claim her. No waiting. Not much longer, anyway.

Dash slid back down her body, wide shoulders spreading her thighs. He lapped at her slowly, drawing her taste and scent into himself. Perfect. She was utterly perfect. And all his.

No shitty little fleabag would come between them again. He didn't care how many he had to kill. She was his.

Colette's thighs tightened around him the moment he brushed his tongue against her clit. He sucked the tiny bud between his lips, drawing and lashing her hummingbird fast. Her hands fisted in the sheets as she started her descent into bliss.

He drove a finger into her, then a second, pumping into her wet heat as a preview of what was to come. She ground down on him, seeking more than he gave her.

"Sweet fuck, Colette," he growled. She'd be his undoing. That was just a simple fact in his life. "Do you know how good you taste? How fucking hard you make me with just your scent?"

She writhed underneath him, pressing herself against his mouth. There she was. Wild bear. His wild bear. Nothing could keep her down for long. Not even the threat of being torn apart.

Dash growled against her soaked flesh. The

sound, the vibrations, grew a tiny moan from Colette. More. He needed more of that noise.

Needed to feel her quake around him.

Needed to see red flush her skin.

He sucked and licked at her with utter abandon and pushed her on with his fingers. He trailed a hand up her side to cup her breast and roll a nipple between his fingers. He wanted to touch everywhere. Lick and nibble every inch. Work every spot that made her pant with need.

"Scream for me, baby," he murmured. "Tell me how much you want this for the rest of your life."

"Dash," she moaned. "Yes. Want. Always."

It wasn't about owning her body or demanding her pleasure. He wanted to show her how much he loved her and wanted to see her happy. All the whimpers and moans made him swell with pride.

He did that for her. He made her feel good.

His cock throbbed in time with her sharp pants. His lion rolled through him. More. He wanted everything she offered.

He wanted to claim her as his mate.

She bucked against him, her body greedy and grasping at his invasion, coating his tongue in her sweet arousal. Her nails bit into his head, his shoulders, his arms. Each mark made him ache for the permanent one she'd leave when he was done with her.

So close. So fucking close. Easy to drive her over the edge. Easy, too, to hold back and drag it out even more.

They had their entire lives for the back and forth, and right then, he needed to taste her release.

"Dash!" she cried out, body tightening around him.

Her hips rocked against him, chasing the final bit of pleasure. He didn't stop. He licked her back down gently, slowed the pumps of his fingers. Dragged out the final twitches of pleasure until her silver eyes found his.

His perfect mate.

Colette's breath still came hard when the room spun. She swayed as she found herself straddling Dash, but she shouldn't have worried. His hands on her hips held her steady.

"I want to watch you move." He cupped one of her breasts, rolling the bud of her nipple until she squirmed. His other hand grabbed the base of his cock and lined up with her sex. He rocked his hips slowly, coating himself in her liquid heat. "Let me watch you come, baby."

She bit her lower lip as he filled her slowly, steadily. Each delicious inch stretched and burned with a pleasure so intense she didn't know how she'd ever survived without him.

His head fell back and his throat bobbed with a hard swallow. His muscles strained with all the movement he contained, letting only his fingers tighten on her hips.

"Fuck, baby," he groaned low in his throat. "You feel so good."

He opened his eyes slowly. Dark hunger stared back at her. Gold swirled with the grey, quickly overtaking the stormy color.

Colette pressed her hands against his chest, lips parting slightly. She swirled her hips in a slow circle, then rose up an inch before falling back down his length. Heat built in her core, more and more with every delicious sensation and tiny movement.

He gripped her hips, guiding her movements at first, urging her to take more of him. A low growl worked out of his chest every time their bodies met, the noise turning to a constant purr of pleasure that stroked down her spine.

Fuck, she loved this. Needed it. Somehow he'd

known exactly how to piece her back together. He didn't take a single thing from her. Instead, he let her have the reins and enjoyed the hell out of it.

Dash threw his head back, eyes churning gold and never settling anywhere. He watched her tits bounce, his cock disappear inside her, her face. His fingers dug into her thighs as he thrust his hips to meet hers, control fraying.

A growl rumbled in him as he pushed off the bed, arms wrapping around her as he held them close together. He moved her on him, never losing the momentum that had her panting with need.

"Colette," he murmured against her skin. "Tell me what you want."

"I want you," she whispered against his mouth. "I want this."

"You have me, baby," he growled back. "You've always had me."

And wasn't that the truth?

He'd waited for her and always held out hope that their connection was the truly powerful, fated kind that spun people back into each other until the moment was right. She'd been at the end of her rope when she came home to Bearden, but Dash had been waiting. He tossed her another line to haul her back into his arms.

Harder. He pulled her against him harder. Faster. Every breath pulled a growl from him, a groan from her. Pressure built in her middle. The peak was in sight, so close she could almost reach out and touch it.

She slid her hand to the back of his neck and held him close. "Dash," she groaned. "Need you. Do it now."

He nipped at her skin, but it wasn't enough. Wouldn't be enough until he sank his fangs into her skin and marked her as his. She wanted his bite as much as she wanted to give him hers.

"Dash," she ground out in a growled rebuke.

He chuckled, the rich sound drawing her body tight. He fucked into her harder, pressing her pleasure higher and higher, until she clenched around him.

"Dash!"

"Come," he growled.

Like she'd been waiting for the order, her body shattered around him.

Pain and pleasure spiked as one, rolling outward from her center. It seared her, burning her from the inside out. Claiming her as entirely as the man marking her as his.

Colette turned her head and bit down on his skin.

Dash roared, head thrown back, neck straining as he throbbed warmth into her.

They moved together, drawing aftershock after aftershock from each other, until Dash fell back and dragged her down with him.

His hands ran up and down her back, soothing her into a boneless heap. "Mine," he whispered against her fresh mate mark.

A shudder passed through Colette. She bit her lip to hold back the high moan that wanted to escape. "Yours," she agreed. "Now and forever."

But then, she'd always been his. She'd just been too stubborn and afraid to admit it.

Dash showed her there wasn't any reason to be afraid. She didn't need to live her life according to the mistakes made by her father or the insanity that gripped Jason. She was her own person, free to make her own choices.

And she didn't have to do it alone.

"So, what do you think?" Gavin Kincaid asked.

Colette eyed the man without moving. He wasn't anything she'd expected. Nice jeans, shirt tucked in, clean boots. If she'd met him on the street, she would have pegged him as someone parading around in nothing more than a costume.

Hell, she hadn't expected him, at all.

He was young, probably not older than her brother. And entirely green about the business.

Still, she'd followed along while he pointed to spots where he wanted the ranch house, the barn, offered possible ideas for dividing up pastures. And now he looked at her expectantly.

Colette stepped away from the man and passed another look over the rolling hills. "The land is good.

It's sat vacant for all this time as a measure to keep a line between the human towns and the enclave, though I'm sure you already know that. You'll be starting from the ground up. Whatever you're budgeting, triple it. Everything will go wrong, then those fixes will go wrong, too. You'll have delays with construction, you won't get the best cattle, and your crew is going to see you as a city-slicker who doesn't know a damn thing he's talking about."

Gavin's mouth twitched, but he didn't let the smile take over his face. "Money isn't the issue and I think you're giving it to me easy with the triple prediction. I don't want to go bust. We can build the herd up slow, get our feet under us."

"We?" She turned to him. "Us?"

"As you've politely told me, I don't know a damn thing I'm talking about, and that includes my neighbors. I need someone who knows her shit when it comes to ranching and this area. If you're willing to come on board, that is."

She blinked, then shook her head. He didn't disappear. He didn't laugh in her face or call a hidden camera crew to reveal themselves. Clear honesty sharpened his scent, and he looked at her expectantly again.

"I would love to," she answered.

Gavin held out his hand. "Then it's a deal. I'll have employment paperwork sent to you this week."

Colette nearly bounced in her seat on the entire drive back home. The offer was everything she could hope for and didn't require uprooting from Bearden, which had quickly become a requirement. She didn't want to pull Dash away from the Crowley pride. Hell, she didn't want to leave them, either. They made her feel like she belonged.

Plus, it let her do the work she loved with the added bonus of not working with Dash. As much as she loved the man, working together day in and day out would result in her jumping his bones or ripping out his throat. Best to have a little extra space to breathe.

And when Ethan and Tansey's cub was born... she would be close for babysitting and cuddles.

Colette bumped along the ranch road, then nearly slammed to a stop. She wondered if she'd taken a wrong turn, but no. She distinctly remembered the signs telling her to GO AWAY and FUCK OFF. They made her snort every time she saw them.

So who the hell owned all the vehicles parked around the dens?

The mystery solved itself the moment she pulled to a stop in front of the den she shared with her mate. Tables and chairs had been pulled out of individual homes. A selection of finger foods were already being picked over by the small army that milled around, drinks in hand.

Her brother and his mate were there. Hell, the entire Ashford clan had shown up. Tawny, too. Dash winked at her through the windshield before turning back to say a final word to Seth and Trent.

"Colette Ashford," Dash called, twitching his fingers for her to join him the moment she slid out of the cab. "Get your ass over here."

Ethan muttered something under his breath that had her narrowing her eyes at him. "What was that?" she growled as she passed.

Tansey shoved an elbow into his side and answered for him. "Nothing," she laughed. "He said nothing. He will continue to say nothing."

Damn straight.

Colette slid her hand into Dash's and found herself tumbled over backward in a sudden dip-turned-kiss that curled her toes. "What's all this?" she breathed when he set her back upright.

"Just go with it. How was your meeting?" he asked softly.

Colette nearly purred. In the middle of the dramatics, he took time to check in with her. He proved several times each day how much she mattered to him. "Guess who gets to tell some city boy how to build up his ranch?" She pursed her lips, fighting to keep the grin off her face. "You're not going to feel inadequate now that I'm more important than you?"

Dash smirked down his nose at her. "Aw, you can be the breadwinner, baby. There's enough equal opportunity to serve back in our den." He pressed a small kiss to her temple, then gestured wildly to the rest of the crowd before she could say another word. "Okay, you fuckers know why we're here. It's somehow become tradition to give thanks or whatever, so thanks for showing up when you were needed. I don't know what I would have done if I lost this amazing, strong, gorgeous woman who makes every damn second of my day better than the last."

Her heart swelled. Such simple words, in such an offhand manner, but they were all true and all Dash. Wild man, caring man, he hopped from fight to fight and never slowed down. She didn't have time to worry about anything when he kept her focused on enjoying all the moments they had together.

Love wasn't the poison she'd watched consume

her father. It wasn't obsession or madness. It didn't tear a person down.

Love built up a person and added to their life. Dash didn't take anything away from her. He made her better.

"Really, though," Dash continued, "you should be thanking us."

Colette ducked her face against his shoulder and tried not to laugh.

"Who offered you a chance to let your claws out? We did. Who proved, once again, who the toughest pride in existence is? We did." He threw an arm over her shoulder and hauled her close to his side. "No offense, bears, but she's ours now so you don't count.

"Eat up, fuckleheads! Dash and Colette, out."

Dash spun her away from the others. Someone, she couldn't tell who, started to clap, but cut themselves short when no one else joined in.

Rude. That was one hell of a speech.

He cracked open a beer and handed it to her before grabbing one for himself. Colette leaned her head against his shoulder and watched the others mix and mingle, split apart and reform into fresh groups. They were all her people, now. Ashfords, Crowleys, she was glad she'd be able to watch both clan and pride grow.

"I'm glad we're staying," she said quietly.

Dash clinked his bottle against hers. "Me too."

Ethan cleared his throat on the other side of Dash. He grimaced at his boots, then turned narrow eyes on her lion while Tansey studiously didn't watch from a small distance away. "I take it I don't need to tell you not to hurt her, lion."

"You didn't need to, but you did." Dash took her brother's hand, then dragged him close. "I'm more scared of her than you, bear."

Ethan barked a laugh. "Then you're not as dumb as you look. She chose well."

Dash turned then and flashed her a smile.

Everything was perfect.

SETH STARTED the walk down the ranch road and toward the barn. His barn, he'd taken to calling it in his head. One he shared with all the horses and any calves that needed extra tending.

He tried not to let it get to him, being so far from the others. What had he expected? An entire damn den to magically appear next to all the others?

No, the living situation wasn't a problem. It was

all the crap in his head, whispering the same dark shit he'd heard for years growing up.

Unwanted.

Wrong.

Disgusting.

Living away from the others—logical as it was, no fault on anyone—still hit him hard despite fighting back against those insidious words.

Seth growled to himself. Assholes. His old pride was filled with assholes. *They* were the wrong ones. *They* were disgusting. He'd found his brother. He'd made a place with his people. Bearden didn't give a fuck who sired him, what blood ran in his veins, or how big and brawny the beast under his skin was. All the Crowleys cared about was getting the damn job done with minimal fighting.

He could manage with that. He could enjoy a life like that.

Except… those damn words lingered in his head and soured him as the night went on.

He didn't want to ruin the fun for anyone. Nor did he want to face the discomfort when they realized what he was.

Shiftless.

ABOUT THE AUTHOR

Cecilia Lane grew up in a what most call paradise, but she insists is humid hell. She escaped the heat with weekly journeys to the library, where she learned the basics of slaying dragons, magical abilities, and grand adventures.

When it became apparent she wouldn't be able to travel the high seas with princes or party with rock star vampires, Cecilia hunkered down to create her own worlds filled with sexy people in complicated situations. She now writes with the support of her own sexy man and many interruptions from her goofy dog.

Connect with Cecilia online!
www.cecilialane.com

Wild Fate

Bucking Fate

Shifters and Sins (BAD Alpha Dads)

Whiskey and Wolves

Tequila and Tigers

Bourbon and Bears

Made in the USA
Columbia, SC
07 May 2020

96518270R00198